D1526422

It All Started at the Masquerade

Janice Cole Hopkins

Janice Cole Hopkins

Other Books by Janice Cole Hopkins

The Appalachian Roots series

Cleared for Planting – book one
Sown in Dark Soil – book two
Uprooted by War – book three
Transplanted to Red Clay – book four

(Slight connection but not a series or sequel)

When Winter Is Past
With Summer's Songs

The Farmers trilogy

Promise – book one
Peace – book two
Pardon – book three

Standalone

Mountain Mishap

For I know the thoughts that I think toward you, saith the LORD, thoughts of peace, and not of evil, to give you an expected end.

Jeremiah 29:11

Chapter One: Invitations

Winton, North Carolina, 1795

Melanie Carter hurried down the dust-laden street. The women's society meeting at church had run later than she expected, and Constance and her brother wanted to meet with her before dinner. She looked at the fierce June sun overhead. It must already be around eleven o'clock, and William didn't like to be kept waiting.

Gemona scurried along at some distance behind Melanie, trying to keep up with the younger girl's quick stride. At thirty-two, Gemona remained in good health, but she wasn't accustomed to moving this fast.

At times like his, Melanie wished she were but a child, so she could run at top speed, but a young lady nearing twenty years of age could do no such thing. However, she made her pace as brisk as she dared, and rushed into the house winded from her hurry.

"They're in Mr. Carter's office," Shadrack informed her, his black eyes filled with worry.

"Have they been waiting long?" She handed him her bonnet and gloves.

"'Bout fifteen minutes I's guess."

"Mercy. Fifteen minutes would seem like fifteen hours to her brother, and the fact he had chosen his office instead of the library didn't bode well at all. This must be a serious matter indeed. Despite the fact the door stood open, Melanie paused to catch her breath and entered the room with all the grace and deportment she could muster.

"Well, it's about time." William sounded impatient but not angry. "Have a seat."

"How was your meeting?" Constance never failed to evoke the niceties society required.

"Too long."

William smiled in agreement, but Constance frowned, no doubt thinking Melanie too abrupt and honest. She looked down at her hands in an effort to diffuse her plain speaking.

"I have some good news," William began, but she looked up to find his and Constance eyes guarded. "Lott Jenkins has asked to court you."

Melanie sucked in a deep breath to keep from reacting too hastily. "But he must be at least forty."

"Yes, but forty isn't old, and he's still handsome and quite virile." Constance sounded pleased, but William's gaze said he thought his wife had overstepped the line of propriety.

Constance must have caught her husband's expression. "Don't fret, William, dear. No one could be as handsome or strong as you, but you're quite taken. By me."

Melanie shuddered from Constance's saccharine show and tried to steel her expression to reveal nothing. Surprisingly, her dour brother looked pleased.

Constance turned back to Melanie. "He will make a fine husband."

For someone else maybe. "But he doesn't interest me."

"Then get interested." William's tone said he would book no argument. "To be honest, we need this match. You know father left the estate without proper funds, and the crops haven't been as bountiful as I had hoped over the last two years. We are hanging on, but the family needs you to make an advantageous marriage. We're counting on you."

Melanie looked at her brother as he talked. He had much darker hair than she, but it still held a hint of red, although his darker brown color hid it better than Melanie's lighter brown did. She'd always hated her nearly red hair – actually fully red in the sun. And where William's eyes were a grass green with just a few flecks of gold, hers were a deep, almost royal blue, much too dark for her coloring in her opinion. At least someone would be hard put to find any freckles. For that, she could be thankful.

William was twenty years older than Melanie. He had been her parents' firstborn and she their last. There had been five babies between them who had never made it to school age, most being stillborn or dying after only a few days.

"Won't Constance need me near in case your prayers are answered and she adds to your family?" The couple had been married for ten years, and Constance had yet to expect their first child. People had begun to whisper about her barrenness, but the couple hadn't given up hope, and Constance kept saying she wanted Melanie around for that event.

By the expression on their faces, especially William's, she knew she'd said the wrong thing. However, she couldn't recall the words.

"What does one have to do with the other?" William sounded even more impatient with her than before. "You can court Jenkins and even marry him and still come back for a confinement and all. He can come, too, as far as that goes. In fact, it will be more suitable for you to help out if you're married."

Melanie wanted to give a hundred reasons why she found the thought of being married to Lott Jenkins unsuitable, but she knew better. Instead, she sat waiting. She could express her true feelings with Gemona and be herself with her companion, but she needed to be retiring and appear biddable around others, even though she often found it hard.

"I did give him my permission to court you, Melanie. He's much more suitable than that Askew boy who's had his eye on you. Toby might have been a good playmate growing up, but he wouldn't make you a suitable husband. He's the youngest son of seven, so he will always remain poor by our standards, even if his father is a successful farmer to some degree."

She didn't want Toby courting her either, although she saw him as a friend. However, of the two, she'd rather have Toby courting her than the arrogant, egotistical Mr. Jenkins.

"Just permission to court you," Constance added. "He's not asked for your hand yet, and he might decide you're not the woman he wants."

Again, Melanie remained silent. The three of them knew permission to court indicated the man would be looking toward marriage. Melanie didn't need to state the obvious.

"Oh, yes!" Constance exclaimed as if she'd just remembered something of utmost importance. "More exciting news. We've just received invitations to attend the masquerade ball the Dickinsons are giving in Edenton in October."

"That's a long way off."

"Not considering how many people they've probably invited, and it will take some time to get the replies from everyone. After that, they'll have all the planning and preparations to do. Besides, we'll need time to come up with our costumes." Constance's excitement showed. "I've never actually been to a masquerade ball before."

"Yes, well, if you ladies will move your talk about the masquerade ball out of my office, maybe I'll get some work done today." But William gave Constance a loving look which let them know he wasn't upset.

Then he turned his eyes on Melanie. "Jenkins will be joining us for dinner after church on Sunday. I expect you to make a good impression." His eyes hardened. "You'd better not defy me or try to undermine me on this if you want to have any say at all in your future, Mel."

No one but William had ever called her "Mel," and he knew she hated it. She pursed her lips to stop any retort. She turned, leaving Constance to follow after her. Her sister-in-law caught up and grabbed her arm to slow her down. "You know he wants what's best for you."

"It doesn't feel that way. It feels like I'm to be put on the auction block to the highest bidder, and he's doing what is best for business and not best for me."

"Calm down and I won't tell William what you said. Arranged marriages are for the best. Our families have a much better perspective on things than we do. They can see who would suit and who wouldn't. Look at William and me. Our two families arranged our marriage, and I couldn't be happier."

Although arranged marriages were what the better families expected, some allowed the young woman to have a say and to have veto power. She doubted if

William would. Both he and Constance always thought their way best, and they would never consider another option.

Melanie gave a quick nod to acknowledge Constance's words. No use in arguing anyway. She'd just need to put the situation in God's hands and do a lot of praying between now and Sunday, five days away.

"Are you all right?" Gemona asked Melanie as soon as she entered her room. The maid, Melanie refused to think of her as a slave since she considered her a friend, sat repairing a rip in a dress Melanie wore for outdoor activities or ones in which she might get dirty and expected no company.

Melanie huffed, fell onto her divan, and proceeded to tell Gemona about what she'd just learned.

"That man ain't near good enough for you." Gemona had long imitated Melanie and spoke without the usual slave dialect, but she still let incorrect grammar sneak in, especially when she became agitated. "You deserve someone to treat you special, and he'll want you to do all the treatin' and cater to his every whim instead."

Melanie sat straighter. "Do you know something I don't?" Slaves were privy to information others wouldn't know, because their masters treated them as if they weren't there and hid little. The slaves also gossiped frequently when they got together.

"Just talk about his womanizing ways and his cutthroat business practices. But he is wealthy and maybe he's ready to settle down. 'Bout time, I'd say."

Melanie smiled at the woman's directness. "I'm glad you're with me. I don't feel so all alone knowing I have your support, and it's good to have someone to share my true thoughts with."

A big grin spread across Gemona's face. "I'm glad to be here. It's good to have a kind, gentle mistress to work for."

"Do you ever regret not getting married or having a family of your own?"

"Not often. You are my family, Miss Melanie. You are the child I never had, my little sister, and my best friend all rolled up in one. Whoever you marry better take me along with you or I'll be one unhappy woman."

"I'll see to it, Gemona, for I feel the same way." But could Melanie be sure of that? She didn't feel sure of anything right now.

Saturday came with a flurry of activity. William told Constance to impress Lott, and she intended to do just that. Melanie shook her head. If President Washington had been coming to dinner, Melanie didn't think Constance would have tried any harder. She felt like a sinking ship in the midst of a fierce Atlantic storm.

Constance turned her scrutiny on Melanie. "What are you wearing to dinner?"

"I haven't decided." That seemed to be the safer reply.

"I wished we'd had time for a new gown, but alas this came up much too quickly."

"Indeed it did." Melanie could certainly agree with that.

Constance's stare grew harder. "You don't seem overly excited. Why this could seal your future."

That's exactly what Melanie feared. "I've only seen Mr. Jenkins from a distance, so I thought it prudent to wait and see how things go."

"Well, William says he's a personable fellow and oh so rich. I think you will be pleasantly surprised."

"I hope so." She would pray that God's will be done. She certainly didn't want to find herself in a bad situation, and from what Gemona had said, that could very well happen if she ended up married to Lott Jenkins. However, in all fairness, she should give the man a chance. It would not be evenhanded to prejudge the man based on hearsay.

"Come." Constance led the way upstairs. "Let's see what we can come up with for you to wear and have Gemona start dressing you well before the time you think necessary. I want no holdups and nothing skipped."

Melanie looked at her sister-in-law. She would have been pretty, except for a sharp pointed nose that gave her a severe countenance much of the time. Just because she was fifteen years older than Melanie didn't give her the right to act as a mother, did it? But then, living in her and William's household did. Perhaps the time had come for her to marry as her family and friends had been pointing out over the last four years.

All during the church service Sunday, Melanie tried not to think of Mr. Jenkins and the impending visit. She knew he would likely be in the building somewhere, but he must be sitting near the back, and she didn't want to crane her neck and be so obvious in looking for him.

However, Constance's continued fidgeting and nervousness did little to keep Melanie's thoughts where they should be. She closed her eyes and said another prayer.

She heard the priest read, "And shall not God avenge his own elect, which cry day and night unto him, though he bear long with them?" God must be telling her she hadn't wearied Him at all. Now, if He would just direct her path and show her what to do about Lott.

"Mr. Jenkins has asked William if you can ride home in his carriage," Constance whispered to Melanie as soon as the service ended. "Gemona will ride along, of course, or I could go if you prefer."

"I wanted to hurry home ahead of him and freshen up." It was the only thing Melanie could think to say that Constance might understand.

"That makes sense. I'll have William inform him."

Gemona had come down from the church's balcony ahead of Melanie, and they left as soon as William joined them in the carriage. Gemona rode with the driver, although William permitted her inside the carriage on certain occasions but not usually when he rode there.

"You go freshen up, Melanie, but don't take long." Constance's anxiety hadn't dissipated. "William will keep Mr. Jenkins entertained until you come down, but dinner will be delayed until you arrive."

Melanie nodded and hurried upstairs. Truth be told, she both dreaded the start of this event and wanted to get it over with as soon as possible.

She didn't take long. Gemona put a couple more hairpins in her coiffure, straightened her skirts, and brushed the hem. "I'll be praying for you," her friend said as she turned to leave the room.

"Good. I have a feeling I will need all the prayers I can get."

"Here she is." William and Lott stood.

Lott was taller than most men, just under six-foot, Melanie would guess. His broad shoulders spoke of fitness, and his light gray eyes reminded her of tin. She couldn't be sure of his hair color, since he wore a wig, and she wanted to laugh. Most men had ceased to wear the monstrosities, as had the Europeans, and not everyone had worn them outside of government and formal affairs in the first place. She thought it looked ridiculous.

Stranger yet, William now also wore one. How had he managed to don that before Lott arrived? Since she and Lott had never been formally introduced, William did the honor.

"This is such a pleasure, Miss Carter." Lott's eyes danced in amusement.

"My family has been looking forward to your visit, Mr. Jenkins." Not exactly the niceties she should express, but she hated lying.

Constance stood. "Shall we make our way to the dining room? Dinner is ready to be served."

William and Constance led the way, and Melanie had no choice but the take Lott's arm and follow. It felt muscular and hard, making her want to pull away and put distance between them.

Since the dining table held twelve, and only four would be eating, William sat at the head of the table, and Constance sat to his right. Melanie sat across from Constance with Lott to her left.

Since Lott turned to her often, she noticed his eyebrows and eyelashes were a pale yellow, reminding her of the inside threads on new corn. Would his hair be the same color?

Only a few faint wrinkles lined the corners of his eyes and lower center of his forehead. Melanie supposed most women would find him attractive. She couldn't decide what she thought about his unusual appearance, and she'd like to see him without the wig before deciding.

Melanie didn't think the table had ever seen so many courses before. She only picked at her food, but the dishes kept coming.

"Aren't you hungry?" Lott asked. For some reason, his observant nature irritated Melanie.

"I'm eating more than it looks like." She had taken at least one bite of everything, and that would add up.

"I like a woman who doesn't overindulge in food or drink." She didn't think his comment needed a reply.

The meal took forever. William and Lott kept the conversation going, with a question or comment to the women only now and then. Lott never appeared ill at ease no matter what the topic, switching smoothly between business, politics, and local affairs. However, Melanie would have been more impressed if he had shown a human side, an uncertainty.

Finally the meal ended, and the small group started for the parlor, but Lott stopped. "I noticed a lovely area behind your house. Might I interest you in a stroll, Miss Carter?" He looked at William for permission.

"Go up and get Gemona and your parasol." Constance gave the answer as she often did, knowing that William would be quicker to nix the idea if he didn't fully approve.

Gemona appeared with a parasol in hand before Melanie got to the stairs. She had the uncanny ability to do that sometimes.

Melanie didn't carry the cumbersome accessory nearly as often as she should, but she welcomed it this time. If she worked it right, she could use her parasol to put some distance between her and Lott as they walked.

Chapter Two: Courted

Lott offered Melanie his arm even before they left the house. However, she took her hand back to open her parasol after they got outside. Lott had to dodge its spread.

"Here. Allow me to take that for you." He reached for the parasol, and Melanie could hardly refuse him. He stepped closer and held the device over her head. "Now, that's better."

"Tell me about your family, Mr. Jenkins." In all the table conversation, there had been very little personal information given.

"My parents are deceased, like yours. Our family, also small, consists of myself, the oldest; my sister, Claudine, who is married and lives in Wilmington; and my younger brother, Henry, who is now in his last year at the College of William and Mary. As a lawyer, he will probably locate to a larger town."

"Where do you get your given name? I find 'Lott' rather unusual."

"It's the surname of a grandfather. Do you like it?"

"I do." She decided to be truthful, and his expression looked so hopeful she could answer no other way. "God saw fit to save the Lot in the Bible from destruction."

He chose to ignore her reference to the Bible. "I find 'Melanie' unusual, too, but I love it. It fits you – soft, easy-to-say, and pretty."

She ignored his flattery. "Although I believe the name has gone out of vogue in recent years, it dates back to the Middle Ages."

"Interesting. How did you find this out?"

"Mother's family were academics, and her father had an extensive library. I've inherited their love of books and, to a lesser degree, research."

He looked surprised. "I've never had the time to do much reading, other than for business."

She tried to keep her expression emotionless, but she so loved to discuss books and ideas. Shallow conversations would only satisfy her for so long.

"I don't remember seeing you at church, Mr. Jenkins. Do you not attend often?"

He cleared his throat, as if giving himself time to search for an answer. "Probably not as often as I should, since I do some traveling in my business. I buy or contract to ship produce and goods. I've also been visiting some of the other denominations around, but I think you will be seeing more of me at your church now." His smile told he felt pleased with his answer.

They walked in silence for a while, but Melanie didn't find it as uncomfortable as she had feared she might. Constance had been correct in this, too. She found Lott quite personable.

Gemona followed along at a discreet distance, giving the couple some privacy while still performing her duties as chaperone. Lott entirely ignored the other woman, and Melanie tried to give the appearance of the same.

After walking for a little over thirty minutes, in a circular pattern, Lott led them back toward the house. "I have enjoyed this time alone with you, but I'm sure I should take you back to the house since this is our first meeting. I don't want to raise any eyebrows, especially your pretty ones. I never thought I would appreciate red hair on a long-term basis, but I've changed my mind. Everything about you is lovely, and I would like to see you again soon. I appreciate your quiet, reserved ways. You can carry on a conversation, but you don't see the need of chattering all the time. I find you quite refreshing."

"Thank you. I've found the day to be a pleasant one as well, and I've enjoyed your company." Melanie found that remarkably true. Their time outside hadn't been nearly as strained or stressful as she had expected. But had she just encouraged him too much? She didn't want to give him false expectations.

"Good. Let's go in and see when your brother will let me see you again."

Lott stayed for another hour with the decision made that she would see him again Wednesday evening. He asked to take her to a newly formed Baptist prayer meeting. She found the concept interesting. Their Episcopal Church didn't have such a thing.

Melanie found Gemona waiting in her room. "How did it go?"

"Much better than I expected. He seems pleasant enough."

Gemona frowned. "Remember, he's putting forth his best face now, and he'll be making special efforts to impress. It won't be the same after you're married." A grin spread across her face. "Did you see that gaudy wig? However did you manage without bursting into laughter? Do you think he wore it to cover his balding?"

Melanie hadn't thought of that. "I don't know. Have you learned that he has a bald spot?"

"No, but it wouldn't surprise me. At forty-two, the man is old enough to be your father."

That brought Melanie back to reality. "I dared not ask how old he was, and I would have guessed he's in his late thirties."

Gemona snorted. "Still too old for you in my opinion."

Melanie didn't care that much about age, but she needed to stick with her original plan and take a wait-and-see attitude. Hopefully, time and God would reveal what she should do.

Monday morning a young lad delivered a dozen red roses to Melanie. The card read, "I keep recalling the wonderful afternoon spent with you, and I can't wait until Wednesday to be by your side again. With warm regards, Lott."

Constance looked at the flowers longingly. "They likely came from his gardens on his estate. I understand his are much more extensive than our feeble attempt."

"We are closer to town, and therefore have less room. If you wanted to move out to the plantation, it used to have a beautiful garden when the family lived there."

Constance shrugged. "I prefer town life, and the plantation isn't so far out that William can't still see to things. His overseer is dependable as well. Besides, since the main house burned a few years ago, building a new house would be a bigger expense than we can afford right now."

Another reminder that they needed Melanie to make a lucrative match. She shrugged off the pressure, and went to find a vase for the flowers. After arranging them to her satisfaction, she placed them in her bedroom. She did love the smell of roses.

"La-tee-da," Gemona sang sarcastically when she saw the flowers. "I bet I can guess who sent those."

Melanie laughed, dismissing the barb. "I only have one suitor."

"And he's tying hard, I see." Gemona's face turned serious. "Don't let fancy ways influence you, for, unlike

Constance, I know those won't hold meaning to you for long. Look beneath the surface to the true man."

Melanie nodded. That's what she wanted to do, but her boat appeared to be in a swift current right now, and it was hard to get her bearings. *Lord, be my anchor, I pray. Show me Thy will and Thy way.*

Tuesday, Lott sent her a silk fan, much too expensive a gift for such a brief acquaintance. Gemona had been right. Lott's attention had gone overboard.

Melanie had the delivery boy wait this time, and wrote Lott a note of thanks for the two gifts. She tried to convey such gifts were unnecessary in her tone, but at the same time, she didn't want to seem unappreciative. It constantly felt like she walked a fine line with this man, and they'd only been together one time.

Lott called for her Wednesday evening and led her to an impressive coach pulled by matching white horses. How could she let him know his lavishness made her uncomfortable? For some reason, it prevented her from relaxing and just being herself. She didn't work hard to make a favorable impression on him, and his extravagance inhibited her. She wished he'd just be himself and not rely on outward appearances.

Lott handed Melanie in to one of the seats and put Gemona across in the other seat. Then he climbed in beside Melanie.

"The Baptists are much less formal than what you're used to," he told her. "I wouldn't want to lose the contacts I have with the Episcopal congregation, but I thought this would be a good diversion for us, and I know you enjoy going to church. However, these folks don't have a building but normally meet in homes. They've been meeting in Hugh Powell's house most recently, and that's where we're going tonight."

Melanie glanced out the window so Lott wouldn't see her nervousness. It would have been nice if Lott had told her exactly what to expect before now, but she couldn't voice her concern without seeming rude or shrewish. "I do like attending church. Thank you for trying to please me," she said instead.

"Always, my dear. Always." She shifted in her seat at his condescending smile.

Maybe Gemona had been wrong about Lott only wanting her to please him. She looked across at her maid. Gemona appeared to be falling asleep and paying no attention, but Melanie knew better.

Sitting close beside Lott in the dining room felt strangely intimate. The table had been removed and chairs pulled in to accommodate everyone. About twenty-some people must have been in attendance.

She looked around and didn't recognize many people she knew by name, although she knew William would have known most of them. She did a second look when she saw Toby Askew. She didn't know he would be interested in a Baptist prayer meeting. He noticed her about the same time, and the glare he gave Lott made her withdraw her eyes and turn them elsewhere.

It appeared Lott drew strong reactions. Constance and William strongly supported him. Gemona and now Toby didn't like the man. Now if she could just figure out how she felt.

She turned to look at him. He hadn't worn the wig, and his pale, yellow hair grew straight and thick. He had it caught with a narrow cord at the back of his neck, but no bald spot could be seen.

He must have felt her gaze, because he turned to her. "Like what you see?" He tried to smile to make it a joke, but for the first time he made her uncomfortable.

She felt her face grow warm, another thing to hate about her reddish hair and fair coloring. She blushed easily.

"I do like you better without a wig," she dared to say.

First, his eyes grew wide, and then he guffawed. "Do you now? I never dreamed you would be so outspoken. Now I can't determine which I like better – the quiet, submissive lady or the bold woman who isn't afraid to speak her mind. You are full of surprises, but I like that. A man would never be bored with you."

That made her blush all the more. She turned to look straight ahead, avoiding Lott on her left or Toby to her right.

She'd learned one thing, however. She'd not try to verbally spar with Lott Jenkins. The man's tongue could be lethal.

Although Melanie could see some positive attributes in Lott, he didn't engage her affections. He seemed too intentional, too calculated, as if he followed a plan set on wooing her. In other words, she never felt she got to know the real man, and until she did, how could she come to care for him?

The summer became a flurry of activity. She saw Lott two or three times a week when he didn't have to go away on business. Constance insisted she have some new dresses, and that entailed countless decisions and fittings. Thankfully, Eliza, Constance's maid, and Gemona were both good seamstresses, because neither Constance nor Melanie had that talent. Widow Sanders took in sewing, but the quality of her work left much to be desired.

In addition, Constance had already started to discuss their costumes for the ball in Edenton, and she wanted Melanie to make her decision about what she would be wearing soon in case they needed to order masks or something else the shops in town didn't carry in stock. William would make plans for their travel to Edenton and back.

Melanie had long enjoyed the warmer months for long strolls and pleasant times outside with a book or just talking with Gemona, but she'd had little time for that this year. All this hustle and bustle didn't suit her at all.

"Melanie! Melanie!" Constance called as soon as Melanie stepped out the back. Her sister-in-law had become more demanding as of late and monopolized her time just as much as Lott.

Melanie turned and re-entered the house. "Here I am."

Constance brisk stride brought her quickly. "William just gave me the most wonderful news." She paused to catch her breath. "Lott has procured a ship to take us down the Chowan River to Edenton for the ball. Isn't that marvelous?"

"Yes, quite." But she knew her voice held no thrill. Maybe once this ball was over, things would settle down some. Now if she could just settle the situation with Lott.

She couldn't be at all sure about him and feared he would never make her a good husband. He had been solicitous to a fault, but he seemed to be holding back and presenting only a partial image of the true man. Here lately, the more she saw of him the more misgivings she had, and he had done nothing to win over Gemona, who usually accompanied them on their outings. However, William and Constance kept pressuring her to bring the man around and accept his proposal once it came. Sometimes she wondered if they wouldn't force her to wed Lott, even if she refused.

Constance gave her a disappointed stare but turned and left Melanie to her thoughts. She sat down on the bench by the back door.

Oh, why did her parents die so young? Father would have been much more understanding than

William, for he had nearly doted on her. And Mother would have never forced her into a marriage she couldn't tolerate.

If she didn't see things differently after the ball, she would tell them how she felt. The longer this went on, the harder it would be to extract herself from the situation. A sinking feeling enveloped her. It might already be too late. By October, he would have been courting her for four months, and she would guess that he'd propose before cold weather set in. Why else would he continue to court her? She might be able to hold off the wedding until spring, but no more than that.

Lord, Thou have promised that all things will work together for good for those who love Thee. I am clinging to that promise. Help me and work whatever is best for me, I pray. Amen.

After dinner that day, Constance and William went out visiting, a rare occurrence, and Melanie grabbed her book and headed to the garden. At last, a chance for some peace and quiet. She had just settled on the most comfortable bench, when Shadrack appeared. "Mr. Tobias Askew to see you, Miss."

"Where is he?"

"Waiting in the entrance."

"Send him around here to the back, but don't come with him. He knows the way. Instead, find Gemona and send her out immediately. "Yes, Miss Carter."

Melanie wished the slaves would just call her Melanie when they were alone, but they refused, saying they might forget so it would be better to always do the proper thing.

"Toby." She stood to greet her friend. "It's so good to see you."

"Is it? I thought you might not want to see my face since you've now moved up to more noteworthy friends. Or should I say suitors?"

Her mouth almost fell open. "It's not like you to speak with so much sarcasm or venom. Would that I could trade Lott for your friendship and be done with him."

His face softened. "Do you mean that Mellie?"

She saw Gemona hurry outside, but the woman slowed and walked to another bench away from Melanie and Toby, although still within sight. Melanie could see the smile on Gemona's face, saying she approved of Toby much more than she did of Lott.

Melanie sat back down and patted the place beside her on the bench. "I mean it with all my heart. I find myself caught in a large trap, and I'm having a hard time loosening myself."

He sat down and turned to her. "Tell me about it. I nearly fell over when I saw you with him at the prayer meeting. It's taken me until now to find the courage to confront you."

"Oh, Toby, surely not." She put her hand on his arm. "It's just me, and I thought we were good friends. You used to say I was your best friend."

He looked away. "Things are changing as we grow older, and I can no longer be sure of our feelings?"

She pulled her hand away and placed it in her lap. "What are you saying? Do you no longer consider me a friend?"

"I would like to consider you much more." He suddenly looked her directly in the eyes, as if trying to assess her reaction.

She swallowed. She wasn't sure she wanted Toby's courtship any more than she wanted Lott's. She would be happy to leave their relationship just like it had always been. However, the last thing she wanted to do was hurt him, so she needed to tread softly.

She looked at her friend. His sandy brown hair grew thick and tended to wave or want to curl, especially when the air hung heavy and humid. His eyes were a pretty blue, lighter than hers. He wasn't as tall or as muscular as Lott, but he felt familiar and welcomed. "I know without a doubt how much you mean to me as a friend. Beyond that, I'm not sure how I feel. However, I can tell you if you and Lott Jenkins were the last two men on earth and I had to choose one of you for a husband, I'd choose you without a moment's hesitation." At least she knew Toby would treat her well, and he'd be honest and aboveboard with her. One could do worse than marrying a good friend.

He chuckled. "The last two men on earth, huh? I'm not sure if that's a compliment or disparagement. That sounds as if I'm still at the bottom of a long list, but at least I'm ahead of Jenkins, so at least I can take some comfort in that."

She joined in his laughter. "I assure you it's not a long list. In fact, I know of no other men whose names are on it."

"Really? That would mean I'm at the top of the list? Right?"

Melanie wished this conversation over so they could move to more pleasant matters. "At the present time, yes. But I don't think I'm ready for marriage right now. I know I need time to think things through."

He put his hand upon hers. "You know your family's going to expect you to marry soon. I'm sure they'll not let you turn twenty-one without a husband by your side. Shall I ask to call upon you?"

"Not yet. There's this huge masquerade ball in Edenton in October, and Mr. Jenkins has invited us to travel on a ship he's chartered. Constance is so looking forward to it that I know they wouldn't look favorably on you now. If things don't change, I plan on telling Mr. Jenkins we won't suit after the ball. I'll let you know when you can ask William's permission to call, though I want to make it clear that this doesn't mean I will say yes to a proposal of marriage from you. Seeing you, however, should keep other men from asking, and I would look forward to spending more time with you. Perhaps we could even go fishing like we used to."

Toby looked pensive. "This is not exactly what I wanted to hear, but at least it's better than an outright rejection. Do you think your brother would even accept my suit? I'm a hard worker, and I'll give you a good life, but it won't be anything like all this." He waved his hand back at the house. "Would that make a difference to you?"

"Of course, it wouldn't make a difference to me. I haven't changed that much. As far as William is concerned, it might. He says the plantation has had two lean years and father left no capital to see us through those times. That's why he's pushing me toward Lott."

"And that's the trap you see yourself in?"

She nodded. "If you can help me escape, I will be most grateful"

"I'll do my best, and if you could look on me with favor as a potential husband, I will devote my life to making you happy."

Somehow, she knew he would try his best, but would it be enough? His touch didn't repel her, but in no way did it make her heart beat faster or cause her knees to grow weak. Had she read too many novels?

"What are you reading?" Toby nodded at the book beside her.

"*The Champion of Virtue* by Clara Reeve." Would he recognize it as a gothic romance? "It was published in 1777. William hasn't bought any new books since he took over."

"I don't remember hearing of it?"

"Have you read anything lately?" She asked it quickly before she had to launch into a discourse on her current book.

"Not since winter, because I started working with father as soon as we could start the planting." However, they launched into a good discussion of the book he'd read back in the winter, which Melanie had also read.

Toby glanced at the sun. "I'd best get going. Something tells me I shouldn't be here when William gets home."

She nodded, knowing he was right but hating to see him go. "Did you see him and Constance leave?"

He looked embarrassed. "Yes. I came into town for supplies, and I saw them walking down the street. I came immediately, but now I need to hurry or Father won't send me on errands again."

"I'm glad you came. Please come any chance you get. It's always a pleasure to spend time with you." She hoped what she'd said didn't give him a false impression, but she meant every word. She missed being able to spend hours and hours with him like they had as children.

"I'll try. I miss those times, too." He took her hand, gave it a squeeze, and hurried away.

"That boy's in love with you, you know." She hadn't heard Gemona come up.

"Do you think so?"

"I know so. Now, what're you goin' to do about it? He's a whole heap nicer than Lott Jenkins."

"Yes, but I'm not sure I want to marry either one of them."

"Well, you'd better figure it all out soon, or you'll find yourself signing your name 'Melanie Jenkins.' You're on a fast-moving ship that's gaining speed, and William's done set the sails for Jenkins, and you're going to have to jump ship and take a chance on drowning."

"Toby did teach me how to swim when I was about seven years old." Melanie cracked a weak smile.

"You hold to that thought. You could do worse than turning to Tobias Askew."

"Do you think William and Constance will allow it?"

"Now that's the golden question, isn't it? Maybe. If you work it just right, but we both goin' have to pray you there."

Melanie put her arm around Gemona's shoulders as they walked back inside, and the woman smiled at her. They rarely got the opportunity to act like friends, but she would always be more friend than slave the way Melanie saw it.

Chapter Three: The Wager

Lucas Hall swiped his hair away from his face and took a deep breath before looking into the mirror to shave. He hated looking at his scarred face, because it always brought reminders of the past he struggled to forget. He wished he could at least grow a beard to cover some of the hideous scars, but no hair would grow there, and he ended up looking worse. Worse? How could anything be worse?

He'd dismissed his valet before coming to this infant country. He couldn't stand the man looking at him, pitying him, and probably spreading gossip. The only person he allowed to see him now was Glenna, and she was more mother than housekeeper. She had been his nanny growing up and thought she knew him better than he knew himself. Sometimes he thought so, too, but not often, and he'd never tell her that.

He performed the task at hand quickly and moved away from the mirror as soon as possible. Strange how the military incident had almost made a different man out of him. He could find little of the once handsome, confident man left. That man had had a secure future, a fiancée, and the promise of a family. This man had none of that.

He completed dressing by rote. What did it matter how he looked, when no one saw him except Glenna? During the day, when his small staff moved about, he either stayed ensconced in his office or his rooms. If he moved about, he wore a mask. Sometimes the mask had a cloth that draped over the right side of his face, but at other times, especially if he planned to go outside, it looked more like a hangman's mask and covered his entire head. He also often wore gloves, since the top of his right hand had also been burned. This way no one ever saw the scars. But mainly he stayed away from everyone, because he couldn't stand their brief stares, or the rumors he knew his appearance created. They had strict orders to look away whenever he came within sight, but some did so much too slowly, and he knew what a curiosity he must be to them.

He went to his office, but hadn't been there long when Glenna came in carrying a letter. "You have mail." She tossed the missive on his desk and sat down in the chair across the desk from him. Sometimes he regretted giving her all the rights and privileges of an older, respected family member. But she was family, the only family he had contact with now. No doubt she waited for him to open the letter and let her know the contents. "It's from Edenton."

"And will you also tell me what it says?" He didn't know why he felt so irritable this morning.

"No, I'm waiting for you to tell me." His snide remark hadn't bothered her at all, and she always gave back whatever he gave her in witticisms. Infuriating woman! But he loved her, and he knew she loved him. The only love he would be likely to have now.

I love you, son. Where had that come from? It couldn't be God. God had deserted him that fateful day on the training field, and he wanted nothing to do with a God he couldn't depend on, not even to keep him safe.

But yet you live. He willed the voice to go away and leave him alone. Everyone else had.

"Well, are you going to open it or just sit there staring at it?" Except Glenna.

He tore through the seal and opened what turned out to be an invitation:

Robert and Mary Dickinson request your presence
at a Masquerade Ball
On Saturday, October 17, beginning at 6 p. m.
Supper will be served
Please r .s .v. p. as soon as possible
And contact us if you have further questions or
plan to stay with us

"Well that's certainly interesting."

Had he read the thing aloud? Why else would Glenna make such a comment? He threw the invitation in the wastepaper basket. "Not enough to persuade me to attend."

"Lucas Hall, you take that out of the trash right now." She used her commanding nanny voice and his full name as well. The military trainers could take a lesson or two from her.

But it only served to stiffen his resolve. "I'm not going."

"Why not? We agreed that you need to get out more. Why, you've become nothing more than a hermit."

"You said I needed to get out more. I agreed to no such thing." He had a stubborn side, too. Whether or not he could be a match for Glenna on this had yet to be determined. Some such battles he won and some he lost. She was a worthy opponent, but she made life more interesting and more tolerable.

"This is your best chance. Can't you see? It's a masquerade, so you can wear a costume that covers your face."

"I know what a masquerade is, but I'm still not going." He would draw too much attention as he traveled back and forth, but he wouldn't voice his concern, because she'd be bound to have an answer for that, too.

"You could even have a private ship take you there and back on the river, and you have several masks that cover your face, if you are so inclined. Frankly, I don't know why you bother. You're not the first person with scars." All too often Glenna seemed to read his mind.

He gave her a look that should tell her exactly what he thought of that idea. As much as he loved the woman, she could be his nemesis, pushing him to do things he had no desire to do.

"Luke, you've become way too self-centered." She tried another tactic.

"Lucas," he corrected. "In this country, I want to be called by my given name and not the previous nickname. I left Luke behind in England."

"That's a shame. There's much to like about Luke."

He raised his eyebrows. "More than with Lucas now?"

Her eyes softened. "I like them both, but I wish I could take the best of both and merge them together. Luke might have been too cocky at times, too sure of himself and his plans, and blind to the faults of those who wanted his attentions."

His eyes narrowed. She treaded awfully close to dangerous grounds, and he'd not allow her to venture further.

"Lucas, on the other hand, has no self-confidence. He's bitter and wants to wallow in self-pity instead of getting on with his life. He has so many good qualities – honesty, integrity, responsibility, caring – but he refuses to share them with others. He refuses to let any woman near him, so she will never know the wonderful husband he would make her."

"Enough!" he bellowed, and hit the desk for emphasis. Not his wisest decision by the throbbing in his hand. "I'll take no more from you."

She stood and glared at him not at all intimidated. "You tried your temper tantrums on me as a boy. They didn't work then, and they're not going to work now. Who else will tell you what you need to hear? You won't let anyone else near you, not even God, so it's left up to me; and tell you I will." She took a deep breath. "You know I only want what's best for you, but I can see you need some time to think things through, and I've got work to do. But don't think this is over. We'll continue this discussion when you've calmed down."

After she exited the room, he shook his head and took a deep breath of his own. She'd left him feeling like that small child in the nursery after a thorough scolding. How did she still manage to have that effect on him?

By dinnertime he felt contrite and ready to make amends. He didn't plan to change his mind about going to Edenton – that should be his decision to make and not Glenna's – but she shouldn't have to put up with his tirades either. The loyal woman didn't deserve that from him.

"Eat with me," he invited when she brought the noontime meal to his suite. She often joined him, but he could see she hadn't planned to do that today. He only ate supper in the dining room after the staff had left for the day.

"I'll be right back." Her voice took on that cheerful lilt he liked.

Thankfully, Glenna didn't mention Edenton as they ate. The smart woman knew when to leave well enough alone. However, he had no doubt she would bring it up again. She always did what she said she would. That's one thing that made her such a successful nanny.

Lucas pushed back his chair from the supper table and smiled at Glenna. Things almost seemed back to normal. One thing about Glenna, she rarely held a grudge.

"Why don't I help you clean up here, and then we can play a game of Put to pass the evening?" The cook left their cooked meal for Glenna to serve, but all the staff went to their nearby homes after six, and he finally had his house to himself.

Glenna raised her eyebrows. He'd never offered to help her clean up before, and Luke would never have even thought to do so. "What? We're not in England anymore, and I'm no longer a lord. It won't hurt me to become a little more plebeian or common acting. Besides, if I help, we'll have more time for Put."

"I wish we could play something with a little more class, like whist."

"I'd like that better too, because it has more strategy, but whist requires four players.

"Are you trying to bribe me by helping me clean up? You know I don't like to play Put with you, because you always win. That's no fun."

He grinned. "It is for me."

"If you're so sure of your winning, why don't we sweeten the pot and make a serious bet?"

Glenna wanting to make a bet? This he couldn't believe. "I thought you didn't believe in gambling."

"God told me I could make an exception this one time, and we won't be betting money."

The woman must be delusional if she thought she'd talked with God. "What then?"

"If you lose, you'll attend the ball in Edenton."

He took a step back. He hadn't expected this. "And if I win?"

"You name your price."

"You will never again hound me to do anything I don't want to do."

"All right. It's a deal."

She agreed to that awfully fast. He felt a moment of doubt, but he shook it off. He would win this easily. As she had said, he always won; and the games were rarely even close.

Lucas threw the cards down on the table and schooled himself not to throw something else. He didn't want a repeat of his earlier outburst. "How did you do that?" Glenna had won handily, and she never won.

"I told you, God was on my side."

He looked closer to see if she might be joking, but she looked serious. Crazy woman!

"You need to go to that masquerade ball. I'm not sure why, but I just know you're supposed to go."

"You're going to be the death of me."

"No, I'm going to give you your life back or die trying." Her face grew somber. "I'm sixty-two years old, Lucas. I'm not going to be here for you indefinitely. I don't want you to spend the rest of your life secluded in this big house all alone. You deserve better than that."

"Yeah, well when have I ever gotten what I deserved? Did I deserve to have the cannon blast do this to me?" He gestured toward his scars. "Did I deserve to have Margaret Ann run in disgust? Did I deserve to have my older brother die without leaving an heir, my middle brother become the duke, and my former fiancée marry the Hall with the better title?"

"No, you didn't, but you can see the good in some of it and rise above the others. At least you know Margaret Ann never loved you but only your looks and your status. When a better opportunity came along, she took it. Charles did give you this estate and all the funds that went with it. And, as for your scars, you now know who your true friends are if you'd give yourself a chance to make any."

"I can't take the repugnant looks I get." He couldn't get the words out above a whisper.

"You shouldn't set such store in what others think. The ones who turn away aren't friends worth having or people worth knowing. You have me, and I love you. And God loves you, too."

He snorted. "Yes, God loves me so much that he had you win at cards for the first time ever just so I'd have to suffer."

"No, God loves you so much He wants you to come out of your self-imposed prison and live again."

"I'm going to bed." He'd had enough of this. Maybe in sleep he could forget it all, if he could sleep.

"And you'll be going to the Edenton ball." He could hear the amusement in her voice, but he didn't turn around. He would be going to the dreaded ball, because he wouldn't renege on a bet or go back on his word no matter how much he wanted to. He should have heeded Glenna's long ago advice and refrained from betting, especially when paying up would be so difficult for him.

As the summer waned and fall approached, Lucas's anxiety about the ball grew. Just the planning of getting there and back and keeping his scars hidden seemed insurmountable. At least, he'd talked Glenna into handling his costume with the understanding it would completely cover his face. He not only wanted to hide his scars at the ball, but he wanted to be unrecognizable. Being the mystery man appealed to him. Besides, wasn't that what made masquerades so enticing? Now, if he could just pull it off.

He got out of bed and looked outside as the morning broke the black of night into the gray of sunrays yet unseen. He threw open the window and breathed in the fresh air, so different from that which always hung thick and heavy in the summers. He loved this time of year, maybe even more than spring.

Today would be a good day for a ride, the one outside excursion he still allowed himself. But his expansive estate had enough land he could do this without taking unnecessary risks of being seen.

He had Glenna order the cook pack him a small breakfast and his horse be brought to the back and tied there. He'd wear his mask until he got out of sight, but then he'd take it off and ride with the wind. The burst of freedom always left him exhilarated and lifted his mood.

After his breakneck race through an open field, he rode down to the river and turned Jester upstream. He could actually have one of his ships dock adjacent to his land to pick him up and take him to Edenton. Then, he'd plan to spend his nights aboard the ship while there. He didn't keep one for his use, because he traveled so seldom. In fact, he hadn't gone anywhere since coming to North Carolina.

Maybe Glenna had a point. Perhaps he needed to get out more, but not too far out. He looked at the river, wide and deep. He'd come down one morning and go fishing. It had never been an activity he'd enjoyed in the past, but the idea of sitting before the river in the early morning now pleased him. Luke Hall may not have enjoyed the solitude or fishing, but Lucas Hall would.

Thursday, Lucas found himself riding out again, this time with his fishing tackle. He had considered walking, but it would have been a lengthy trek from the house, and he wanted to be able to make a hasty escape should anyone come trespassing. He found a log, pulled it nearer to the edge of the water, and began to prepare his line.

He'd spent time reading up on the sport over the last couple of days, since he didn't know that much about it. He had crated up much of his extensive library and brought the books with him on the voyage from England, but he'd added to them all along. Since becoming a recluse, he needed his books.

He had overseers and managers that ran his businesses, and they required little effort on his part, nothing that couldn't be taken care of by mail. He did keep an eye on the accounts, however, and that kept him busy.

Sitting by the river didn't give him the sense of freedom that a fast ride did, but it proved more calming, and he needed that now, particularly with this ball coming up. He looked around. He might even go hunting some this winter. He needed to enjoy his property more, and the walls could be confining, even in a fifteen-room house.

Chapter Four: Fishing

Melanie knew what she needed to do, but that didn't mean she wanted to do it. Since Lott was officially courting her, she had to tell him about Toby's visit, but she didn't think Lott would welcome the news. She tried to look on the bright side. At least this would give her a much better idea of her suitor's true nature.

She chose to talk to him Sunday afternoon in a private moment when they walked in the small garden. "I had a friend come by and visit last week."

"Oh? Who was it?"

"Tobias Askew. We practically grew up together."

"A man! Isn't that more than a bit improper, since you've accepted my courtship?"

She made sure to keep her voice calm. "He's just a friend, more like a brother really. He didn't come courting."

"Why did he come?" His voice had hardened.

"Just to visit a friend. His father sent him into town for some supplies, and he had time for a quick visit."

"Were William and Constance here?" Why did he have to ask that question?

"They'd gone out momentarily, but Gemona stayed nearby like she is today." She glanced back at her maid.

"I don't like it." He stated the obvious. "In fact, I'll not have you seeing other men."

She wanted to tell him she would not have him dictating who she could or could not see, but she dared not. Most men expected their women to be obedient, William included. However, she saw this as a very dark blot against Lott.

"Does it not matter that I came to you with the news?"

She saw some of his stiffness relax. "It does, and I appreciate your honesty. However, that doesn't change the impropriety of it. You can't have another man calling on you and have my approval."

"Lott, he really didn't come to call on me in that way. He knows that you are courting me. In fact, we talked about it."

"Can you honestly tell me you'd never consider him as a husband?"

"I can. Not unless my hand was forced in some way. He's just a friend from my childhood, and more like a brother nearer my own age."

"Then make sure he stays in the past and don't see him again. How old is he, by the way? I know his father, but there're so many children, I don't remember them all."

"Toby's twenty-two, about two years older than me."

"Toby is it? Stay away from him. Promise me if he calls again, you'll be unavailable." He looked at Melanie, expecting a response.

She swallowed. "I'm not sure I can make that promise. He said something about going fishing for old time's sake. Of course, we'd be well chaperoned."

His face turned red with anger. "I'm not at all sure that fishing is even appropriate for a young woman like you. And I take back every thought I've ever had about you being meek. You need to learn to do as you're told or you'll never make a decent wife."

"Does that mean you're discontinuing our courtship?" She hoped her voice didn't sound as eager as she felt.

His livid expression told her she should have never asked that question. From the corner of her eye, she saw Gemona move closer.

"Not on your life." He pushed it out from between clenched jaws. "You will be my wife, Melanie, and you will be taught to obey me. I always get what I want one way or the other. Always."

Melanie took a step back, afraid that he would reach for her shoulders and shake her. Instead, he balled his fists by his sides. She didn't know if he did so to keep from shaking her or if he planned to hit her. His stare cut her to shreds before he turned abruptly and stormed away.

"Good riddance," Gemona said beside her. "Too bad it's not likely to be permanent."

"Y-you don't think so?" Melanie hated how her voice quivered. Lott had upset her more than she thought.

"Not according to what he said, and I don't think that man would ever give up. It would be admitting defeat, and that's one thing Lott Jenkins will never do."

Constance and William fumed over what she'd done. At first, she just told them she didn't want to discuss it, but that didn't work out well for her. When she explained, she got two different reactions. William told her she must do as Lott wished and quit seeing Toby altogether.

Constance wanted to know why she had told Lott to begin with. "You should have kept that information to yourself and not volunteered it. What were you thinking?" She said this out of William's hearing.

"I wanted to be honest and not keep secrets. I thought, as my suitor, he had a right to know."

"You'd better put those thoughts out of your mind. When you marry Mr. Jenkins, you're going to need to keep some secrets."

Melanie had never noticed this side to Constance before. And the fact that she said "when" Melanie married Lott and not "if" spoke clearly. *Lord, am I doomed in this matter?*

Melanie didn't see Lott for two weeks after their argument, and she felt set free in those two weeks. Regrettably, it didn't last. On Friday, she received a note from him:

Dear Melanie,

I have had business concerns that demanded my attention, but I'm going to be free Sunday. I shall plan to see you in church, and perhaps you will invite me to spend the afternoon with you. I look forward to seeing you after this long interlude.

Sincerely,
Lott

She clutched the paper until it crumpled, tempted to throw it into the fire. He gave no regrets for his behavior and no apology.

Constance came into the room and saw the note in her hand. "Is that from Mr. Jenkins?"

Melanie nodded, and Constance took it from her hand to read. "Good. I see he's ready to forgive you."

Forgive me! Melanie barely caught the words before her tongue spit them out.

"You must write to him and invite him to Sunday dinner after church. It will be good to have him calling again. I had begun to fear you'd run him off."

How Melanie wished she had. At one time she'd been unsure about Lott. Now she knew for certain he would never suit, and she could not marry the man.

She looked at Constance's determined face. She didn't know how she would extract herself from this situation, but, by the grace of God, she would. Somehow, someway, she would. She had to.

She wouldn't mind being obedient to a husband she could respect, a God-fearing man filled with integrity. Lott Jenkins had just proven he was not such a man.

Toby sent her a note Saturday, and Shadrack managed to get it to Gemona without Constance's or William's knowledge. The staff knew much more than William or Constance would ever have guessed, and they all were on Melanie's side.

She sat down on the divan in her bedroom and opened the note. It read:

My Dear Melanie,

From some of the rumors I've heard, I'm afraid I may have inadvertently caused you trouble by visiting. That was not my intent, and I've been praying for you. However, I did promise you a fishing trip, and I want to be a man of my word.

If you are so inclined, meet me at our spot on the river early Monday morning. If you think this not wise, I will understand. Just send me word so I will know.

Your friend,
Toby

"You need to go," Gemona said after Melanie shared the note. "You shouldn't let Lott dictate your every move and not allow you to see friends you've had since you learned how to walk. And Toby might prove to be a help in getting out of Lott's grasp. You never know."

"You're right. We're not married and not even betrothed. Yet, I've accepted his courtship, at least in all appearances, and I don't feel right meeting another man behind Lott's back."

"How do you consider Toby when you think of him?"

"What do you mean?" Melanie couldn't very well answer the question when she didn't understand it.

Gemona tried another approach. "If I didn't know him and you were introducing Toby to me, what would you say about him?"

"I'd say, 'I'd like for you to meet Tobias Askew, my longtime friend.'"

"Do you have any romantic interest in Toby?"

"N-o-o, but why all these questions?"

"If you just view Toby as your childhood friend, and you aren't interested in him otherwise, I don't see anything wrong with meeting him to go fishing. Chaperoned by me, of course."

"Even if I agreed with you, I doubt William would let me go."

"Just tell him you and I want to go fishing. He'll likely send one of the men with us, but if you catch him when he's busy, I don't think he'll protest too much. He remembers how you used to do this all the time. Now, Constance is a different story. I wouldn't mention it to her until after the fact."

"I never realized how devious you can be."

Genoma gave an unamused laugh. "You've never needed my deviousness like you do now. If you get away from Lott's claws, you may need much more than a little manipulation and subterfuge. I'll never forget what he said to you that day in the garden. He's determined to have you for his wife."

"I won't do this without telling him I saw Toby. That would feel like cheating, and I'll not be that underhanded or dishonest."

"Then, you make sure you're in William's company when you tell him, and then don't spend any time alone with him for a while afterwards. That man scares me."

As Melanie started to implement Gemona's plans, she had misgivings. This didn't feel right. Could that be a sign that God disapproved. She prayed for clarity, but she had none.

Her brother pulled her off to the side Sunday night as she started to retire. "I have some businessmen coming by Monday morning, and I might be tied up most of the day, certainly all morning. Constance is getting together with a group of women at a friend's house, and I'd appreciate it if you could make yourself scarce until dinnertime. Some of these men don't have the best reputations."

Strange that it would be William to put Gemona's plan in motion. "Gemona and I had been discussing going fishing. Would that be all right?"

"I thought you'd outgrown that, but I see no harm in it. I'll send Jericho with you," He had already turned away before she could reply.

Lord, since this turned out to be so easy, I hope this is Thy will. Now, if Thou will just work on Lott so that he decides I'm not worth his time and trouble and says good-bye without causing problems.

Melanie awoke when Gemona came into her room from the adjoining closet where she slept. She squinted her eyes as Gemona lifted the candle higher. "Is the sun up?"

"It will be by the time we get ready."

Melanie stretched, trying to shake off her morning drowsiness. "It won't take long to get ready to go fishing. Just put on old clothes and roll my hair into a knot."

"And pack some breakfast for all of us, take a jug of water, gather the fishing tackle, and find Jericho."

None of that would take long, but Melanie didn't say anything. Truth be told, she felt ready to get out of the house and sit down by the river.

They had too much to carry, so they decided to take the small wagon. Jericho had suggested the cart, but that would really be reverting back to childhood, and someone would undoubtedly poke all sorts of fun at her, maybe even Toby.

Although they arrived at Toby's favorite fishing spot earlier than Melanie had imagined, he waited for them. The smile on his face welcomed her warmly. "I hoped …."

"Fancy meeting you here." Gemona interrupted Toby before he could finish his sentence.

Melanie knew she did it to cover the fact that they'd planned to meet him here. Toby gave both women a hard look but said nothing.

The four of them busied themselves getting things organized and set up. Toby and Melanie took the closest log for their seating, and Gemona and Jericho moved downstream a few yards to another downed tree trunk. Large trees grew profusely around the river where they hadn't been felled for docks or landings.

"What's going on with Gemona?" Toby asked when they'd gotten their poles baited and into the water. He always brought their bait.

"She's trying to protect me and make it look like we met you here by accident."

He looked a little pale. "I hope this won't cause you additional trouble. I heard Jenkins quit seeing you for a while from his anger over my visit."

Melanie knew gossip carried fast, but it surprised her that this piece of information got out. The house slaves must not be as loyal to her as she had thought, although Lott could have been the one to talk. "I wish that's the way of it."

He raised an eyebrow, and she explained. "I would be happy if he would quit calling at all. But he informed me that I wouldn't get rid of him that easily. He intends to marry me."

"Then you aren't favoring his suit?"

She shook her head, not wanting to go into all the details.

A grin spread across his face. "That's the best news I've heard in a long time."

"Don't get too excited. I don't think my resistance will deter Lott, and Constance and William favor the marriage."

"But he hasn't asked you yet?"

"No. I know Constance has hinted to him to wait until after the ball in Edenton to propose. I think if someone with more money and better social standing were to ask for my hand, Constance might shift her support and persuade William to do likewise, but that's about the only way. And I can't see that happening."

She stared out at the river. The burden of it all pressed down upon her. The more time that passed, the direr her plight seemed to get.

Toby startled her when he reached for her hand. "We'll think of something. You could always elope with me."

He said it casually, but she could tell he meant it. He had a good heart, and she wished she did have romantic feelings for him.

"It would be hard to get away from the three of them long enough to wed, and where would we go?"

"I'm not sure, but I could check and see where we might get married right away without waiting." His voice sounded hopeful, almost joyful.

"I'll keep that in mind if things become desperate. Thank you." She squeezed his hand and then pulled hers away. She knew she'd hurt him by referring to marrying him as a last resort, but she would hurt him more if she gave him false hopes. He deserved someone who could love him completely.

He turned the conversation to other things after that, and it did seem like old times. Melanie had missed these times. Growing up left much to be desired, especially for a woman.

The fish were biting, and they caught enough to feed both families before the sun moved directly overhead. Toby walked Melanie to the wagon while Jericho put their things in the back.

"Thank you for this, Toby. I needed this time of peace, and I can't remember when I've enjoyed a morning more."

"I'm glad, and I could say the same. We're compatible, Mellie. I'm serious about wanting to marry you. I know you don't love me the way I love you, but I'll be so good to you, you'll come to love me." He handed her up into the wagon.

She leaned her head down. "I'll always love you as a dear friend, Toby. No matter what happens, that will never change."

"I'll be praying," he called as the wagon rolled away.

"That man is in love with you," Gemona said after the wagon had pulled from the sight of Toby.

Melanie looked at Jericho. He kept his eyes on his task of driving the wagon, but she knew he'd heard. She wished Gemona would delay such conversations until they were alone.

"I'm beginning to realize that." She sighed, struck again by the fact that Toby would likely get hurt. She would, too, if Lott had his way. As if her thoughts had conjured up the man, she looked up to see him riding toward them.

Chapter Five: Underway

Lott's body had stiffened and his face hardened by the time they drew close enough to talk. Melanie put out her hand to tell Jericho to stop the wagon, but she didn't take her eyes off Lott.

His eyes swept the wagon and landed back on her. "What are you doing out here dressed like a vagabond?"

"We went fishing this morning." Surely he could see the poles and tackle in the back.

"Ladies of quality do not go fishing." He emphasized each word.

"I used to go often as a child, and William approved of my excursion this morning." She looked down at her hands, hoping to give the impression of being humbled and thus placating his disapproval to some degree.

"Well, I do not. It's unseemly. I hope you didn't bait your own hook." He looked at Jericho and back at her hands.

She met his gaze, sat up straighter, and stuck out her chin. "I did, and I took the fish off as well."

"Are you nothing but a common wench?" His fists clenched. "Perhaps I should have forgone courting you and taken you for a tumble in the hay."

Too shocked to speak, Melanie felt violated by his words. How dare he speak to her in such a vulgar way! "And you are no gentleman."

She felt sure he would have hit her if Jericho had not been present. The slave's robustness couldn't be hidden as it pushed at his clothing.

"Mr. William won't take kindly to you disparaging Miss Melanie that way." Gemona shouldn't sound so educated in front of Lott. Thankfully, he ignored the slave.

Lott looked at Melanie with contempt. "We'll just see about what he thinks." Lott motioned for them to continue on, and he turned to follow.

When they arrived, Lott stormed into the house. It appeared that William had just stepped from his office with a man Melanie didn't recognize. Something about the stranger's appearance looked seedy to her.

The man shook William's hand. "If you decide you need to sell any more of your slaves, just let me know."

William looked none too pleased at their intrusion. He likely didn't want anyone to know he needed to sell off some of his slaves. Melanie hoped none of the house servants would be affected. Hopefully it would be the field hands housed out on the plantation, but she hated that thought, too.

"Jenkins." The man nodded to Lott as he walked by with Shadrack standing ready to open the door.

Lott gave a reciprocal nod and turned to William. "I found Melanie coming from the river looking like a field hand herself. She says you gave her permission. What's this about?"

William straightened to attention, the frown on his face growing deeper at Lott's abruptness. "Why don't we go into the sitting room, since my office may feel cramped with the three of us?"

"Now, to answer your question," William continued with his eyes on Lott. "Melanie doesn't like being confined to the house all the time, and she enjoys going to the river, epsecially on a hot summer's day. She and her friends used to go there often. I didn't want her around this morning with this business I needed to conduct, and I gave her permission to go fishing. I see nothing wrong with that. I assure you the activity didn't taint her, since it never has, and she's still just as much a lady as ever. You should appreciate that Melanie isn't the simpering idiot so many young ladies are these days."

Lott must have realized his error, for he changed tactics. "Maybe you're right. Seeing her so poorly dressed and realizing she'd just been handling night crawlers, fish, and such unnerved me at first."

William leaned forward and looked at Melanie with a smile playing around his eyes. "Melanie is unusual, and the man who marries her will be lucky indeed. But, since your appearance is less than satisfactory to our friend here, why don't you go up and change? I'm sure dinner is about ready to be served. You will join us, won't you, Jenkins?"

"It would be my pleasure."

"If you will excuse me then." Melanie stood to go to her room, but then she paused. "I think I should also tell you that we found Toby Askew fishing this morning, and we joined him. And Jericho brought home enough fish for cook to prepare for supper."

She saw the hard look return to Lott's face before she fled to her room. Thankful that she'd had the opportunities to inform Lott of meeting Toby at the river in William's presence and the fact that she had a reason to leave the room immediately, she hurried to tell Gemona what had happened. She could do this while she freshened up and changed clothes.

"I've told Melanie she's not to see Askew." Lott's voice held much more venom than William had ever heard before.

He observed the man in front of him. He needed Mel to marry money or they'd lose the house in town and who knew what else. Constance would not fare well

in the overseer's house on the plantation, and he
wouldn't be able to afford anything better until the
accounts made an upward turn, if they did.

But at the same time, he'd never seen this hard,
domineering side of Jenkins before. The man had always
been a polite gentleman in the past. Would he be doing
Mel a disservice to unite her with him for life?

He'd never realized what a balancing act being the
guardian for a young woman could be. Melanie should
have married several years ago, but she'd not found
anyone to interest her, and he wanted her to be happy.
Now, here she'd almost become a spinster, and he
needed her to make a good match. He tried to tell
himself this is what families with their standing in
society did, but that didn't entirely alleviate his
misgivings.

He'd just sold off two of the house slaves and five
of the field hands. Outlaw had agreed to wait until the
harvest was in to claim his possessions, but William
could tell the plantation had not produced enough this
year to see them through the entire year until another
harvest. If Melanie married Lott, his brother-in-law
would help him get the estate affairs on a firm footing
again. With the right investor, William felt sure he could
get everything shored up and flourishing again.

"And when did you tell her this?" William saw that
he'd left Lott's question hanging for much too long.

"The day she told me Askew had come to visit her
here."

"Toby is a childhood friend. He and Melanie grew up together and even shared a tutor for a time. He's a good lad. I see no harm in her seeing him on occasions, with a chaperone nearby, of course."

"You don't see it inappropriate for her to be courting two men at once?" William could tell Jenkins tried to keep his anger from erupting, but it simmered just underneath the surface.

William let his own guffaw burst forth. "Melanie is most assuredly not interested in Toby courting her. In fact, I mentioned him as a possible suitor when she turned sixteen, but she would have none of it. You have no need for worry in that direction. Toby is just a friend. Jealousy does not become you, my friend."

"Nonetheless, I don't like her disobeying me. I expressly asked that she not see the man again, and what does she do? She goes fishing with him."

William didn't know how to reconcile this demanding Jenkins with the man he'd always seen before. He found more and more to dislike about this one before him today. "I think you need to rethink how you get a gentle woman to obey you. If she respects and cares for you, she will want to obey you. But if you feel you no longer want to pursue my sister, we will release you from courting her."

Now, Jenkins sat back as if William had thrown a punch at him. "No. I didn't mean that at all. I'm sure you're right, and it's just that our relationship is new. I trust she'll come around when she comes to know me better and her feelings for me grow."

Happy that issue had been settled without him losing his best prospect for a brother-in-law with deep pockets, William stood. "I think I heard Constance come in and slip upstairs. Let's see if the women are ready for dinner. Shall we?"

William tried not to look at Jenkins too closely, but the brief glance had showed a man whose lips smiled amicably, but whose eyes remained as hard as ever.

Melanie remained as quiet as possible during dinner. She wished she knew what had gone on between William and Lott, but she could tell Lott seethed underneath a polished veneer. At least he gave the appearance of nothing being amiss.

She'd needed to follow Gemona's advice and avoid being around Lott without William or Constance being present. She hoped she would be able to manage it.

Lott looked over at her when they'd finished the meal. "I would love a stroll in the garden, Miss Carter." Although he had watched her often through dinner, he hadn't spoken directly to her before now.

"I'm afraid I'm developing a headache." Her head had begun to pound as soon as they encountered Lott and his wrath. "I believe I'd better retire to my room for a while."

"The fishing must have tired you out." She turned her head away from his smug look, afraid that the retort she wanted to give would only make her look bad in front of everyone.

She took a deep breath. "On the contrary. Sitting by the water in the shade always refreshes me. However, conflict does take its toll."

He raised his eyebrows but said nothing. He looked at her a moment longer with something akin to grudging respect in his eyes. Then he turned to William. "I would like to invite the three of you to my house for dinner Thursday night. I've taken advantage of your kind hospitality on numerous occasions, and now it is high time I return the favor."

Constance's eyes lit up, and William replied quickly. "We'd be delighted."

"Then, since Melanie is indisposed, I'll take my leave. Why don't you come early so I can show you around." He looked directly at Melanie. "Say, about five."

"Until Thursday then, my friend." William shook his hand. Whatever their discussion had been, any disagreements must have been settled.

Thursday turned out to be a rainy day, but it had tapered to a steady drizzle by the time they left for Lott's. Melanie prayed the sky wouldn't clear, which would make it easier to refuse a walk in the gardens. If it did come to that, Melanie hoped she could finagle it so that Constance or William or both would accompany Lott and her. Surely he would be a better host than to leave them alone in the house by themselves.

"You may stay here, Gemona," Constance told the woman. "Since Melanie will be with William and me, we won't need you."

"Yes, ma'am."

Gemona flashed Melanie a look that said this would help keep one of her relatives beside her at all times. Melanie gave the slightest of nods to say she understood.

None of them had ever been to Lott's before, and it turned out to be farther out of Winton than Melanie thought. Not only did the front gate that led up to the house look impressive, but the large, brick house looked more like a governor's mansion.

"Why this is more of a palace," Constance gasped.

"It does look like something transported from Europe." Even William's voice held awe.

Constance tore her eyes away from the house and looked at her husband. "It makes the houses in Winton look like backwater cabins, doesn't it?"

"I don't think our two-story, white home looks like a cabin." William took exception to Constance's remark.

"You're right, dear." She patted his arm in a condescending way. "But our house is like most of the houses of the better families, and many others are rather rustic, don't you think?"

"I'm not sure I agree. The Askews have a decent place, although not as nice as ours. Many such farmers make a good living. Just because most of them use their money to purchase field hands instead of house slaves doesn't make them less successful. Although some of the families around just barely manage to make it, the majority do all right." William looked at the house. "Well, shall we?"

They made their way to the door while Jericho took the carriage around to the back. The butler answered the door and led them to the parlor.

Lott stood, greeted them, and welcomed them to his home. The housekeeper, an older woman with a dour expression, brought refreshments. After chatting for several minutes, Lott showed them some of his home. They didn't go upstairs to the bedrooms, but what Melanie saw looked impressive in a lavish, opulent sort of way.

Melanie lost count of the different rooms, each one unique in some way. The type of woman who set a high value on material wealth would have been enthralled indeed but not Melanie. She preferred a simpler style with less clutter.

"There are eight bedrooms, several with sitting rooms, in the next two levels," Lott said as he led them toward the dining hall. He turned to Melanie. "Which was your favorite room, Miss Spencer?"

"I would have to say what you called 'the garden room.'" The light, airy room had lots of windows, a brick floor, and potted plants in profusion. Even the furniture seemed more cheerful. "I've never seen anything like it."

He beamed. "I'm so glad you approve."

"I also liked the library." Although she'd change the heavy dark furniture if given a chance, she loved the ornate walnut bookshelves that went to the ceiling and the books scattered about on their shelves. She wondered if Lott had read any of them.

They took their seats and were served the first course. As the meal progressed, Melanie found the food tastefully prepared. They weren't served all the courses Constance had ordered for Lott's first meal at their house, but what they had exceeded any of it.

Afterwards, they played whist. She and Lott won handily. When William told him what a fine time they'd had before they took their leave, Melanie could agree. Lott hadn't acted so easygoing since the first weeks of his courtship.

"I have to go away on some business, but I'll plan to see you when you board the ship for Edenton." Lott seemed to be talking more to Melanie than anyone. I believe we are the only two families from Winton who've been invited, but some others from Murfreesboro and Colerain will also be joining us there. I thought some of them might sail with us, and I invited them to do so, but they'd already made other arrangements. I've given William our schedule."

"We'll be looking forward to it," William replied, "and thank you for providing the ship."

Melanie couldn't say she looked forward to it. Although a part of her saw it as an adventure, another part of her dreaded the event. She had a feeling the masquerade ball might change everything, and they could be changes she wouldn't like.

"What am I supposed to do at some masquerade ball?" Gemona's face turned down in a pout. "And I ain't ever been on a ship before."

"You know what to do." Melanie couldn't understand why her normally bold maid had turned fearful all of a sudden. Did she have the same foreboding Melanie did? "You can just do what the other ladies' maids do."

"Slaves you mean?"

Melanie shrugged. "Why are you suddenly being so difficult? As my maid, surely you knew I'd need you."

Gemona nodded. Finally, she'd agreed. "I guess I'm just put out by the whole thing. First, Eliza and I had a hard time getting the dresses and costumes made. Then, Miz Constance is all a tither making sure everything is just so, Toby isn't even invited, and we're to sail on Mr. Lott's ship. We're liable to end up in the belly of a big fish."

Melanie laughed. "He's Lot not Jonah."

Gemona smiled but retorted, "Yeah, well if Edenton burns like Sodom, it wouldn't be much better, and if it does, I'm running as fast as I can and not looking back."

Gemona joined in Melanie's laughter this time, and their silliness seemed to relieve much of the tension. It also brightened Melanie's outlook.

"We need to trust God more in all this." She spoke her thoughts aloud. "Sometimes I get so wrapped up in my perspective I forget to do that."

"You're absolutely right." Gemona gave her an apologetic smile.

With all the activity surrounding preparations to go to Edenton, the day they needed to leave came all the sooner. They packed up and headed out with almost a small entourage. The three of them traveled in the first carriage, along with a minimum of baggage. The servants followed along in a second vehicle with their own things and a bit more luggage. The bulk of their belongings, however, followed in a separate third conveyance. Constance, it seemed, had alone brought more than Melanie and William put together. If Lott had seen all the trunks, he wouldn't have likely invited others to sail with them. If they brought as much, the ship might have sunk before it left the dock.

When they arrived at the dock, they found everything well-organized and working smoothly. Slaves came forward to take their trunks and bags on board. Lott met them on deck, as if he'd been watching for them, and welcomed them aboard. Melanie found herself reluctantly impressed.

The ship wasn't a large one, but it looked well-kept and ready. Despite living near the river, Melanie didn't know that much about ships, and she hoped to get a chance to see and learn more.

Lott showed them to their cabins himself. Gemona and Eliza shared a tiny room off Melanie's cabin. William and Constance would stay in the next cabin down, and Jericho would be below somewhere.

"Come up on deck when you get your things stowed and settled." Lott's words sounded solicitous as he looked at Melanie, but she noticed how hard his eyes still looked. "We'll watch the ship set sail together, but there's no need to hurry. It will take a while to get everything readied."

Melanie nodded. "Thank you, Lott, for providing all this. You've done a fine job of arranging things." She shouldn't be rude, although she wouldn't cower if he became unreasonable again.

Once Lott exited and closed the door, she looked around. The cabin might have been a fraction the size of her bedroom at home, but it looked attractive and comfortable.

Gemona had already begun to put some of Melanie's things away, although her two trunks hadn't arrived yet. Melanie had ended up bringing two to keep from crushing her gowns, but Constance had brought six. Eliza had gone to unpack for Constance and help her freshen up. If Melanie knew her brother, he would be on deck already.

"Here, let me repin your hair." Gemona open the box with the hairpins.

"There's no need. The breeze will just blow it loose again."

"Then I'll just put in extra pins." Gemona had a determined look on her face that said no breeze would defeat her efforts. Melanie sat down and let her maid have her way.

"I sure do wish I didn't have to share a room with Eliza," Gemona grumbled. "We'll have to watch what we say around her if we don't want Constance to know."

"You could come in here and stay with me."

"I don't think that would help, given how clearly I can hear you moving about, even with the door closed. These walls must be paper thin and the doors flimsy."

Melanie understood. "Then we'll just be extra cautious. Perhaps Eliza will be in Constance's cabin much of the time during the day."

"We'll still need to be extra quiet and not talk above a whisper."

Melanie sighed. She didn't like all this secretiveness, subterfuge, and underhandedness. Lott had certainly complicated her life. She just hoped he wouldn't turn her into someone she didn't want to be.

She walked up with Constance. William had told her not to venture out of her cabin without a chaperone.

Sailors weren't known for being gentlemen, although she doubted if anyone would dare be disrespectful to the woman who had Lott's interest. Still, she didn't want to do anything to draw gossip.

The hallway and stairs seemed to close in on her. Melanie didn't remember everything being so tight before, but it had been several years since she had sailed, and this ship appeared smaller. She ran her hand over the rich woods. It had more character than some, however, and she liked all the extra details.

Lott came to her side as soon as she emerged into the sunlight. "How do you find your quarters?"

"Quite sufficient. I like all the efforts to make things attractive and appealing."

He nodded. "It's a smaller ship, but if it suits, I'm thinking about buying it. I've never wanted to get into the shipping business, preferring to be the link between producers and buyers. However, I can see the advantage of having a ship for my own personal use. Since it won't be carrying that much cargo, I'm looking for a smaller one that can navigate the rivers better. Perhaps a wife would like to accompany me some."

Melanie moved to the railing to keep from replying. Nothing about her wanted to be that woman. "How long until we get underway?" she asked to shift the conversation.

"The captain won't be specific, but it shouldn't be too much longer."

Chapter Six: The River Ride

It felt like hours, before the ship set sail, however, it couldn't have been much more than one or two. Melanie had seen Constance return below deck, and William kept glancing her way. Lott seemed aware of this too, so she hoped he would stay congenial, at least in appearance. She sensed him seething underneath his friendly demeanor. Undoubtedly, he planned to bide his time until he had the opportunity to show her his displeasure for her disobedience. Lott wouldn't be the sort to forget something like that.

She sighed. After they returned home from the ball, she would tell William and Constance she could not tolerate the idea of marrying Lott. They wouldn't be pleased.

"Is something wrong?" Lott must have heard her sigh.

"Not really. I'm just ready to get underway."

"I would have never guessed you'd be impatient, Miss Carter." He didn't sound amused or even tolerant. "By the way, don't you think it's time for me to start calling you by your first name?"

"I think it would be better to wait until an engagement before the proper formalities are dispensed with." Had he asked in a less contentious moment, the answer might have been different, but she found his constant displeasure with her irritating and tiring.

She heard an unusual sound and felt the ship begin to slowly move. She looked up to see the sails billowing. She hadn't even realized they'd lifted anchor, a feat she'd meant to watch. Talking with Lott tended to demand all her concentration. She couldn't imagine putting up with the demanding man for the rest of her life.

The ship eventually picked up some speed, and Melanie watched Winton fade on the horizon. She would have liked to ask questions, like how long Lott thought the trip to Edenton would likely take on this ship, but she didn't want to prolong their time together. Instead, she took her leave and turned to go below.

"It's a nice ship, isn't it?" William asked as he accompanied her.

"It is, and Lott says he will likely buy it."

"Really? I think that's a splendid idea. I wonder if he'd allow me to borrow it on occasion." He didn't add "after you wed," but Melanie knew that's what he meant. Could he force her to marry Lott, and more importantly, would he? Surely her brother wouldn't put financial matters above her well-being.

Melanie eventually heard William come back to his cabin. He had returned on deck after seeing her to her cabin. She had lain down on the small bed hoping to nap, but she lay there with the dread of what might be ahead and fear of having to marry Lott building.

She got up and called Gemona to help her don her dress and accompany her upstairs. She hoped that Lott had also gone to his cabin since William had. When she got on deck, she didn't see him anywhere and felt a great burden lift.

Gemona followed her to the railing, but stopped short of touching the rail or looking over the side the way Melanie did. "I don't like this constant rocking or the moaning and groaning of this beast." Gemona's gaze took in the ship. "This is the first time I've ever been on a ship, and I hope it's my last."

Melanie had learned to accept Gemona's contradictions. She could be too forward and bold at times, but then turn cowardly at others.

"I like being out on the river, and I would look forward to crossing the Atlantic if the opportunity ever presented itself."

Gemona shook her head. "You're downright crazy. Give me the ground under my feet any day. I don't take after my Lord, and I can't walk on water. The only way I like the river is when I'm sitting on its banks."

She smiled at the way Gemona expressed her thoughts. God had blessed her when her parents had presented her with the slave. She didn't know what she would do without Gemona as her friend. If she had the power, she would free the woman.

The ship passed by some lovely wooded land with a few clearings before she saw a cleared pasture. She could almost imagine riding a horse across the grass to the river in the quiet of morning.

"I miss riding," she said to no one in particular. She used to ride almost every day when they lived at the plantation, but she couldn't remember the last time she'd been on a horse's back. She needed to ask William to accompany him to the plantation before cold weather arrived. Hopefully, she could maneuver it so Lott wouldn't know about it, or he might want to come, too.

"What's that?" Gemona pointed at a town on the shore.

"That's Colerain." The first mate had stopped behind them when he heard the question. You'll find several towns along the river between Winton and Edenton."

"Colerain. I've always wondered about that unusual name," Gemona said. 'Cold Rain' would make more sense. Is it named for a Cole family?"

"No, it's actually named after the town of Coleraine in County Kerry, Ireland. John Campbell, who founded the town, came from there, and I have a married sister who lives in Colerain."

"Thank you for sharing that information," Melanie told him. He tipped his hat and proceeded on. She remembered the town of Colerain, but she hadn't heard its history.

"I guess we should be going back to the cabin." Melanie didn't want to stay so long she'd be detained by Lott appearing.

Gemona looked up. "I imagine it will be soon time for dinner, and I'm ready. I like being in the fresh air better than down in the hole, but I don't like seeing all this water and knowing I'm at its mercy."

Melanie laughed. "Our cabin is hardly the hole."

Gemona shrugged. "Let's go down and make you presentable so Constance won't be scolding you. I declare your hair doesn't like this river trip any better than I do."

Dinner consisted of a pork stew and sweet potato pudding for dessert, and Melanie could find no fault in the simple fare. Being in Lott's company again turned out to be the worst part of the meal.

The galley and accompanying dining area were small, and only the four of them, along with the ship's officers, ate at the table, but Melanie still found it cramped. In fact, Lott sat so close to her that they often touched, and she tried to keep from cringing. The more she saw of him, the more intolerable he became.

"This stew is quite tasty," Constance remarked.

"I hired my own cook." Lott looked smug or arrogant. Melanie didn't know quite what to call it. "I knew I wouldn't deal with the usual ship's food. I've been forced to do so on too many business trips, and I wanted better for us this time."

"You've done an excellent job of providing for us, Mr. Jenkins." Constance's voice sounded honey-sweet.

"I concur," William added. "I'm so glad you took care of everything, and I didn't have to."

Lott sat up a little straighter, and his chest expanded a little more. "It's my pleasure. I'm used to dealing with business interests, and I know how to get what I want."

Melanie slumped a little lower in her seat. "If you will be so good as to excuse me, I'm not feeling my best. I believe I should retire to my cabin." They had finished eating, although she had no doubt the others would remain at the table conversing for a time. As for Melanie, she'd had as much of Lott's company as she could take for now.

"I hope you're not going to succumb to seasickness, Miss Jenkins." He sounded filled with concern for her, but his eyes held questions about the truthfulness of her statement. The man's acute observations and sharp intelligence frightened Melanie all the more. She hadn't lied, however. Lott's overbearing presence coupled with the all too frequent touching of their bodies had left her queasy, although she had an idea that he did that intentionally much of the time. At times she wondered if he took pleasure in vexing her.

As much as she wanted to go up on deck, Melanie stayed either in her cabin or Constance's for the rest of the afternoon. Constance had developed an unsettled stomach from the movement of the ship and took to her bed. Although Eliza sat with her when she slept, Constance would call for Melanie when she awoke.

Since Constance didn't feel like talking, apart from applying cool, damp cloths to her forehead and holding the basin for her when she needed it, Melanie just sat beside the bed. How she wished she could stroll the deck and watch the sights on shore slowly pass. She liked to feel the wind against her face and hear her skirts flapping behind her. It gave her the feeling of flying, of being free, much like riding a galloping horse did.

It would be best that she remain below, however. She knew Lott wanted to get her alone, since she had defied him by fishing with Toby, and he would consider Gemona inconsequential. Unless William or Constance was present, he would call her to task, and his tirade this time would likely be even worse than before. She hoped the longer she put him off, the more time would erase some of his ire, but she wondered.

Since Constance didn't make it to supper and only the captain came from the crew, the four of them weren't jammed together as before. Given the circumstances, Melanie didn't even mind being the only woman present. She knew William to be the most vigilant chaperone of all from the rare occasions when he'd served in that role.

With fewer at the table, Lott also received closer scrutiny, and he could neither scoot his chair too close to hers nor utter any calloused remarks. Therefore, Melanie relaxed and enjoyed the meal. William's laughter at her witty remarks encouraged her, and she soon had the captain rolling with laughter.

Supper came in three courses. First, they had a fish chowder, as mild as any Melanie had ever tasted. Next came duck roasted in some sort of fruit sauce Melanie couldn't quite identify, along with corn pudding and snap beans, served with a marvelous yeast bread. Finally, they had an apple cobbler for dessert.

Even after the table had been cleared, they lingered with the men having a glass of port and Melanie another cup of tea. The captain looked across the table at her. "You are a delightful, young lady, Miss Carter, and I don't know when I've enjoyed anyone's company more." His eyes went from William to Lott. "You are very lucky men. You, Mr. Carter, for having such a delightful sister and you, Mr. Jenkins, for being allowed to court her."

"You are too kind, Captain." The captain was a tall man in his early fifties, who may have once been handsome, but time at sea had not been gentle. His weathered skin looked leathery, and his thinning, dull brown hair showed plenty of both gray and white.

William chuckled, enjoying the praise about his sister. "Well, being the caring brother that I am, I should see my sister back to her cabin for the night."

Lott looked at her. "Don't you want to stay up to see us dock in Edenton? We should be there before late."

"No, I've found it to be a tiring day, and I want to check on Constance." They were staying on the ship, so none of them would be disembarking until tomorrow. "I'll see you in the morning, Mr. Jenkins."

"You can count on it." Lott didn't sound at all happy, and the captain raised his eyebrows at the rude tone.

"I hope to also see you tomorrow." The captain dipped his head, took her hand, and touched his lips to the top of it. With that, he left.

If Lott were a kettle, he would have been dancing from the steam, but with William by her side, he said nothing.

"Lott seems rather moody at times, doesn't he?" William observed as he walked her to her cabin.

"Much too often, and his moods are often dark or explosive where I'm concerned."

"Well, men often become tense around the woman they want before the wedding. I'm sure his moods will improve once you two are married."

Melanie wanted to scream her disagreement, but she knew better. If she ever voiced anything negative about Lott's behavior, her brother always gave some excuse. He refused to see the bad in the man, and with William, it worked better to ease him around to her perspective. She just hoped she could do that. He seemed blind when it came to any faults Lott Jenkins might have.

Melanie didn't rest as well that night as she wanted, and she wished the ship hadn't docked. Its rocking motion might have lulled her to sleep. Gemona would tell her she's crazy again.

Constance, on the other hand, looked well-rested and fully recovered the next morning. "Are you ready to start our day?" her sister-in-law asked with all eagerness.

"I suppose."

Constance ignored her lack of enthusiasm. "Lott sent word that he had ordered our breakfasts brought to our cabins this morning. I sent him back word that I'd prefer to eat in the dining hall, since I'm feeling so much better, and I missed seeing everyone last night. William just came down and told me he'd changed his mind at my request. Isn't he just the sweetest man?"

"I don't think that's what I'd call him." Melanie guessed Lott wanted to keep her away from the officers, especially the captain.

At first she thought Constance planned to ignore her comment, but then she replied, "Oh, and what would you call him?"

Now, answering that question would be way too dangerous. "I'm still deciding that."

Constance frowned. "I wish you could see the opportunity before you. Lott is by far the richest man in Hertford or Bertie County. And he wants you for his wife."

"I just wished he wasn't so strict or overbearing." She dared not say more, and even at that, she'd likely overstepped.

"You've been spoiled, Melanie. That's your problem. Both your father and then William have been too lenient with you. I imagine Lott has seen this and realized a heavier hand is needed. A husband is the head of a family and you need to realize that."

Melanie bit her tongue, but she didn't argue. It would only make matters worse. "And what are our plans for today again?" Melanie knew them already, but she needed to shift the subject.

Constance's face brightened. The masquerade would take place tomorrow, and they'd have most of today free in Edenton. "We'll go shopping this morning. In light of Lott's interest in you, William has given me an allowance that will allow some purchases."

Now Melanie took her turn at frowning. Why did the topic of conversation usually lead back to Lott?

Constance continued. "We'll bring our purchases back to the ship and eat dinner here. Then we'll change clothes and be at the Dickensons' at three o'clock for tea. There will be other ladies there of course, but I understand only about half of those invited to the ball have received invitations to the tea. I'm just so excited that we're included. Then, of course, the masquerade will begin tomorrow at six. I'm glad we get to go for a visit before then and will have some idea of what to expect. However, I'm anxious that we make a good impression today."

"I'm sure everything will turn out fine." Almost a whole day without Lott's presence. Surely he wouldn't escort them shopping, would he?

He didn't. Gemona and Eliza went to help with purchases. Jericho drove a rented carriage and would also carry their packages back to the carriage as needed.

Melanie enjoyed the morning more than she expected. Although she didn't love shopping the way Constance did, she did enjoy it on occasion, and the Edenton shops had much to offer.

At times, she and Gemona would separate from Constance and Eliza. For example, she and Gemona would go into bookshops or stationery stores, while Constance and Eliza would buy the latest bonnet in an adjacent millinery.

By the end of the morning their purchases had mounted, and the three slaves balanced an array of packages in their arms as they walked aboard the ship. William and Lott stood on deck waiting for them.

"I hope you didn't buy out the stores." William's serious expression belied his teasing tone.

"Not at all, dear," Constance replied. "I didn't go over the budget you gave me, and Melanie only bought two books, some writing paper, and a bottle of ink."

"What? No new clothes or accessories?" Lott looked directly at Melanie.

"I have plenty for now."

"You should have bought some." William sounded bold, almost bitter. "I'm sure Constance spent your part that you didn't."

"You bought me some new clothes recently, William, so I'm fine."

Constance moved toward the stairs, and William followed her. The servants had already taken the purchases down.

Lott moved closer to Melanie as she followed. "I would have been glad to give you some funds for shopping if William is short," he whispered for Melanie's ears only.

She hurried to catch up with her brother. Lott wouldn't buy her affections that easily. "I really don't need anything else now."

"Maybe for your trousseau then."

Chapter Seven: To Edenton

Lucas looked at his housekeeper stunned. "Surely you jest. You can't be serious."

She huffed and puffed up like a setting hen defending her nest. "And what is wrong with your costume. You told me to handle it, and I did."

Well, that had obviously been a mistake. "You expect me to wear a suit of armor? How would I ever maneuver at a ball? The thing must weigh a ton, not to mention how uncomfortable it would be."

"Only the mask is substantial, and I know you'd prefer it that way. The rest of it is lightweight chainmail, not the real thing but made especially for your costume."

He fingered part of it. "How did you manage this?"

"You have a very competent blacksmith and staff."

"I'm not sure the tight-fitting pants are even decent." He decided to try another tactic.

"Now, would I present you with something to wear that's indecent? Surely you know better. Come, try it on. I want to see how it fits you."

Lucas pulled up from his office chair, reluctant for this torture but not knowing how to avoid it. Maybe the garb would fit so poorly he could throw out plans to attend the ball altogether. A man could hope.

The silvery costume fit him as if it had been made just for him, which it had. Why did Glenna have to be so efficient and resourceful? His only stipulation had been that she provide a complete covering for his face, which she had done.

On first glance, he'd been certain the leggings would look obscene, even with the extra pieces of armor, but they didn't. The tunic hung low enough to cover him to below his thighs, and the lightweight armor also hid much of his legs.

"This would never do for a tournament, you know." He couldn't resist the comment.

"Yes, but that's not where you'll be going now, is it? You're just going to a ball."

"Yes, well, it's likely to be much more dangerous to me than combat." However, he dropped his teasing immediately when he remembered that fateful battle that destroyed him. He hoped he'd be proven wrong about the ball.

He didn't ask Glenna how she came up with all this. Frankly he didn't want to know. "Edenton here I come." He sarcastically spit it out with much more venom than he intended, but Glenna smiled anyway. She had gotten her way.

"It's made so you can remove it easily if it becomes too cumbersome."

He didn't reply, but he wouldn't be removing anything. He had been coerced and cornered into attending this affair, but that didn't mean he would stay the entire time or dance at all. No, he planned to go late, after supper had been served and leave early. In between, surely there'd be a garden bench where he could sit in the shadows, and no one would notice him. Glenna might have won the bet, but that didn't mean he would do exactly what she wanted.

At first, Lucas thought about taking his coach to Edenton, not wanting to subject himself to the scrutiny of the sailors on a ship. However, the more he thought about it, the more his mind changed. The coach would be less comfortable, and they would have to push to make it in one day, even if they left as early as possible. Then, anything could happen on the road, and an accident rendering him unconscious would mean losing control of who would see his face. Even a broken wheel would bring unwanted attention and questions he didn't want to answer. On top of all that and even more certain, he'd need a place to stay, and that became the deciding factor.

On the other hand, if he had one of his own ships take him, he could have a crew selected that would likely keep mum about him, and he could pay them extra to do so. They could also be told ahead of time about his mask and his desire for privacy. Plus, he could stay on the ship, foregoing the need for an inn. So in the end, he sent a letter to his favorite captain explaining his requirements, knowing the man would follow his wishes to the letter.

"I wish I could go with you." Glenna looked at him wistfully. "I could stay on the ship during the ball."

Her longing eyes almost made him agree. "I need you to hold down things here."

She laughed. "And will you be expecting a hurricane now?"

He grinned. "You never know." He'd welcome a hurricane if it meant he didn't have to attend this masquerade.

When he boarded the ship, the sailors averted their eyes, and his mood lifted, but he hurried below anyway. He planned to stay in his cabin the rest of the day, and his meals would be delivered outside the door. If everything went well, he could come out and spend some time on deck after dark, when the shadows would help disguise him. Of course, he'd have his cloth mask on, too.

The trip to Edenton went without a problem. He even enjoyed the food, although it couldn't compare to what Glenna and his cook fixed. He didn't expect it to.

That night he stood on the deck looking at dim lights dotting the city. There were too many ships docked here to suit him, but he knew they could see little of him in the darkness. Still, he'd consider it a good reminder to stay below during the day. Tomorrow, he would attend the ball, and then bright and early the next day, he would sail for home.

How he wished he'd won the card games, not just so he wouldn't have had to come to Edenton, but also so Glenna would stop trying to make him be social again. Now, he'd never know when she'd get it in her head to pester him again. He'd make sure of one thing, though. There'd be no more betting with Glenna O'Brady.

"You will learn to obey me." The man's angry voice cut through the night, grabbing Lucas's attention. "And you will marry me. The quicker you learn to accept those two things, the easier it will go for you."

A woman's voice answered in soft muted tones, and Lucas couldn't quite make out what she said. Did the man not know his voice carried on the soft sea breezes, especially when he yelled?

"Your suit would go better if you were more gentle and kind, Mr. Jenkins." That almost sounded like a slave's voice, although Lucas found her diction to be better than most. She must be the woman's maid and chaperone. He let out the breath he'd been holding, glad that the woman didn't face this man alone.

He heard the crack of flesh slapping flesh. "How dare you hit Gemona!" He could hear the woman now.

"She's but a slave, and as such, she will not talk to me like that. If I wasn't afraid of marking your face, I might give you a taste of the same. But then it is a masquerade ball, so perhaps you could cover the bruises with a mask or pretend they are part of your costume."

"I can't believe you. Do you think your behavior will endear you to me?"

"I don't really care. I can see you have been given too much independence growing up and need to be broken. And I do enjoy the breaking. You will become my obedient, submissive wife, giving in to my every wish, and that's a promise."

"Is everything all right here?" Lucas breathed a sigh of relief that someone had come to her rescue. He didn't know what he would have done had the bully hit the lady, but he would have done something.

"No, captain. It isn't. Mr. Jenkins just hit my maid."

"The slave talked back to me, captain, when Miss Carter and I were having a lovers' quarrel. I reacted before I thought."

"Then perhaps you should walk the deck to cool off, sir, and I'll escort Miss Carter and her woman to her cabin."

Lucas heard them leave. He stood thinking for a moment, but then turned to go to his cabin. His time on deck had been ruined by the scene he'd heard played out.

Lucas didn't attempt to go to bed until late, but he still couldn't get to sleep. The events that had taken place on the nearby ship gnawed at him.

Jenkins, Jenkins. Where had he heard that name before? He vaguely remembered someone named Jenkins in the area, but he couldn't pull the recollection to mind. He would eventually, though. Since he'd become a recluse, his memory had sharpened.

Why would the young lady (Miss Carter was it?) even tolerate such a ruffian? Perhaps the man was so rich, she'd put up with anything to marry him. But then she'd stood up to him instead of being submissive or congenial, and she sounded upset.

The threats bothered Lucas more than he cared to admit. Jenkins had told Miss Carter that she would marry him, and he would break her. That last part worried him, because it didn't sound like an idle threat. It sounded like something the bully almost looked forward to. That man needed to be stopped, but Lucas had such conflicting emotions over the matter.

He told himself that it didn't concern him, and he should just forget about it, but himself wouldn't listen. Now, he had begun to sound like Glenna. His housekeeper would be very disappointed in him if he wasn't concerned about the situation, and so would he for that matter. He sure didn't want to become calloused and uncaring like some of the people from his past had been. But what could he do to help the poor woman? Nothing. If he tried to get involved as a grotesque, interfering stranger, he would likely just make matters worse.

You could pray. Where had that come from? He hadn't turned to God since Margaret Ann left him.

Don't you think it's about time? What could it hurt? And it might help that young woman.

It sounded like something Glenna would say, but that couldn't be possible since he'd left his housekeeper back in Colerain. Was it his own conscience? Could it be God?

Lucas turned the words over in his mind. The source didn't matter, but the truth of the message stuck him. It had been long enough. It was time he renewed his relationship with the God who had sustained him before he became disfigured. He shouldn't blame God for Margaret Ann's or his brother's betrayal, and blaming Him for his injury wouldn't change a single scar.

That lady across the way certainly needed his prayers, and, if he were honest, he did, too. He stopped beside his bed, fell to his knees, and did something he hadn't done in years. He prayed.

The short prayer just pleaded on Miss Carter's behalf and for Gemona's healing. But for some inexplicable reason, when he stood up, he felt comforted, as if he'd just met with his long-lost best friend.

He quickly readied for bed and lay down. Despite wondering about Mr. Jenkins, Miss Carter, Gemona, and God, he fell asleep quickly.

Marveling again at the effect praying had had on him, Lucas awoke the next morning and lay in bed with Miss Carter still on his mind. Something nudged at him, but he didn't know what he needed to do. Common sense said he should stay out of it, other than perhaps praying for the woman.

After dressing and eating breakfast, the cabin walls felt as if they were moving in on him. Putting his black cloth mask in place, he made his way to the deck.

A thick fog shrouded everything, and the air hung thick and heavy. He couldn't see the clouds, but knew they must be there. He couldn't even see any of the neighboring ships. Would this murky morning turn into a wet afternoon? His heart sank. That would mean there'd be little escaping the ballroom.

He folded his arms, and his hands touched damp sleeves. If this fog didn't lift, it could be just as wetting as a light drizzle. At least he'd be as well-hidden now as in the darkness of night.

He absentmindedly moved to the side of the ship where he had heard the troubling conversation last night and startled to hear Miss Carter's voice again. "I feel sure William will come up soon."

Lucas shifted his position. Did Miss Carter have more than one suitor? How did she manage that? He should be glad she had an option other than Jenkins, but she didn't seem to make the best choices in men.

"And what if he doesn't. What if it's Lott that appears first?" That was the maid's voice. Lucas couldn't remember her name, only that it had been unusual.

Lott. Lott Jenkins. Ah, yes. He remembered now. He'd been told how ruthless and unscrupulous the man's business practices were. Apparently he dealt with his relationships in the same manner.

"William, could I have a word with you. In private, if you please."

"Now, hold on." Jenkins must have come up, too. "Don't you think you're being rude to exclude me?"

"Not as rude as you were last night, and I need to talk with my brother on a personal matter."

Oh. William was her brother. Lucas didn't take time to examine why that made him feel so much lighter.

Lucas heard Jenkins sputter, but he also heard footsteps walking away. Miss Carter might not be the cowering female he'd assumed.

"William, Lott threatened me last night and hit Gemona when she tried to get him to calm down."

"That's hard to believe. What did he say to you?"

"That he intended to marry me regardless of what I said and that he would enjoy breaking me. Come closer, Gemona. Look at her face. That should be proof enough. Besides, I don't know why you wouldn't believe me. When have I ever lied to you?"

"Lott, would you come here, please."

The man must not have gone far, because it took him no time to return. "Yes, what is it?"

"Did you threaten Melanie and strike Gemona?"

"Threaten your sister? Of course not. Why would I threaten her when I'm courting her and want to marry her? And as far as the slave goes, she talked back to me, and I acted without thinking. I shouldn't have, since she's not even my property, and I do apologize for that."

Lucas clenched his fists. The man was lying. Surely Carter could see that.

"Apology accepted. See there, Melanie. Things aren't as bad as they appear when you hear Lott's side of things. I think there's just been a misunderstanding."

"Why do you always take his side over mine?" Miss Carter sounded near to tears, and Lucas's heart squeezed, "Does his money and influence mean more to you than your own sister?"

"Your reaction's uncalled for. Why don't you go below and try to consider the situation impartially. This dampness can't be good for your appearance, and I know you'll want to look your best tonight. I'm sure you'll see things differently upon reflection."

Miss Carter didn't say another word, but Lucas heard the sounds of her and her maid walking away. He couldn't believe her brother. His sister had asked a good question. Why would he believe a liar over his own sister telling the truth?

Should he go over and tell William Carter what he'd heard? That would be admitting that he'd eavesdropped, and would Carter be any more inclined to believe him, a stranger, than his own sister? He doubted it.

According to his sister, Carter had been blinded by what Jenkins could offer the family. Lucas shook his head in resignation. From what he could tell, she'd been accurate in her perception.

Lucas stayed on deck most of the morning, but he heard nothing else from the neighboring ship except sounds from the crew. By dinnertime, the sun had begun to burn off the fog and mist, and he went below.

"I am so sorry, Gemona. Is it very painful?" Melanie looked at the bruising on Gemona's face and felt like crying. Even on her dark skin, Melanie could see the discoloration and swelling.

"It ain't your fault, so you don't need to keep apologizing. You aren't responsible for what that man does."

"But you wouldn't have said anything to him if not for me."

"I just wished it would have changed Mr. William's mind about forcing you to marry the man. Then it would have been worth it."

"I would've never thought William could be so blind either. He's always been reasonable, and I thought he cared too much for me to take the chance on someone harming me like Lott threatened."

Gemona looked thoughtful. "I think Constance has had a hand in persuading him, and she can see no fault in Lott Jenkins. If she weren't married to William, I think she'd marry Lott herself."

"I wish she could, although, on the second thought, I wouldn't wish him on anyone. Oh, Gemona, what am I going to do?"

"We'll continue to pray, of course. And you're going to go to this ball and have a great time, and the Good Lord willing, you'll gain some Christian man's attention. He'll be even richer than Lott, and you'll end up marrying him and living happily ever after."

"You can't be serious? I'm quickly learning there are no fairytale endings, and the idea of the scene you just described is completely farfetched."

"Don't become so cynical, Melanie. Don't give up hope. Perhaps it's time to give Toby serious consideration."

Melanie sighed. "You might be right. I'll try to talk to William as soon as we get home, but I don't hold much hope that he would approve of a match between me and Toby. Toby comes from a good family, but he doesn't have Lott's wealth or influence. But I will try to talk with my brother."

Chapter Eight: The Masquerade Ball

After another simple meal of ham, cheese, bread, and apples, Constance became intent on getting ready for the ball. "I'm glad we didn't have a heavy meal," she told Melanie as they walked back to their cabins. "I'm sure Mrs. Dickinson will have an elaborate supper, more like a banquet or feast."

Truth be told, Melanie had begun to feel a bit apprehensive herself. Something about this masquerade ball felt monumental.

At Gemona's insistence, Melanie also took longer than usual to get ready. In some regards, it bothered her that they were making so much effort to impress these people. How much more fun it would be if she could just go and be herself. However, since it meant so much to Constance, she kept her thoughts to herself and did what they expected of her.

That's what she really wanted – a man with whom she could just be herself and he'd love her anyway. Lott seemed to try to change her at every turn. Gemona had a point. Toby would make her a much better husband.

Her thoughts swept back to yesterday's tea. She had been worried about going there, too, but she shouldn't have. There'd been so many ladies in attendance that she'd been required to do little more than smile and nod once in a while. In fact, she couldn't remember when she'd felt so invisible. The ball would be at least twice as crowded since the men would also be there, but it would require more of her. How many men would ask her to dance? She hoped Lott didn't plan to dominate her time, but she feared he might.

Despite how ridiculous and unrealistic she knew Gemona's idea of Melanie meeting a Prince Charming who would replace Lott to be, her maid had planted a seed in Melanie's mind that refused to be dug out. Or was it in her heart?

She laughed at herself. She had scoffed at Gemona for having such romantic notions, but apparently she could point the finger at herself now. She guessed she had so little hope after William had taken Lott's side yet again that she clutched at anything. *God help us all.*

Realizing that the Dickinsons would likely have their guests announced, Lucas reconsidered arriving at their house late. He didn't want to be announced when a crowd had gathered, so he arrived as early as possible without being ill-mannered. He'd just have to leave early to make up for it.

"What an unusual costume, Mr. Hall," Mrs. Dickinson told him as he met her and her husband after being announced.

"Only fitting for this beautiful castle." He waved his hand to indicate her home. They both recognized it to be an exaggeration, but Lucas still remembered the flowery language that the aristocrats appreciated.

"Well, welcome to it, and enjoy your evening. The supper buffet will be ready soon, and folks will just go as they please."

He thanked her and moved on, looking for a place he could become unnoticed until the day began to dim and the dancing started. Then he would go to the gardens. It would appear strange for him to be there by himself now.

Glenna and her cohorts had designed his mask so a portion could be moved and he'd be able to eat, but he had no intention of eating supper here. In fact, he'd eaten a snack before he left the ship and ordered a late one for when he returned.

"I'm Edward Smith." A man with graying hair dressed like a pirate came up and extended his hand to Lucas.

Lucas laughed to lighten what he was about to say. "I was under the impression that we weren't to introduce ourselves since it's a masquerade."

"Right you are. Maybe we can introduce ourselves after the masks come off and faces are revealed."

Lucas gave a brief nod to acknowledge he'd heard, but he didn't plan to be here then. He wouldn't stay past ten. Four hours should satisfy Glenna that he'd lived up to his bargain, and he guessed the masks would come off around midnight. He sighed. By all indications this would be a long evening.

Melanie followed William and Constance in on Lott's arm. He'd tried to be more solicitous to her on the way over. She didn't know if he regretted his previous harshness or if he did it in front of William and Constance to stay in their good graces. Either way, she hoped it would make the evening more pleasant.

How she wished she could be paired with someone else for the ball. After the obligatory greetings, they made their way slowly toward the dining room. Melanie didn't feel hungry, but apparently William and Lott did.

On the way, Lott stopped to talk with acquaintances, and he seemed to know a lot of people. He had dressed as a king, complete with royal robe and crown, and the costume suited him. The tailored outfit let her know again how fit and muscular he stayed. Had he learned that she would dress as a medieval lady? Is that why he chose to wear this costume?

He bent toward her. "You look ravishing." She winced at his choice of words. He had already told her she looked lovely, but that had been in the coach with William and Constance in the other seat.

She had worn a green dress trimmed in gold and patterned like those of bygone days. She liked its style, because she found it comfortable and easy to move about in. It would serve well for the long night and dancing.

She only wished she had a gold mask to match. Constance had ordered them both masks that better matched their costumes, but the shopkeeper had warned them they might not make it in time. Therefore, Constance had purchased a purple and a red one, which were the two choices the man had in stock. Sure enough, the ones they ordered did not arrive, so Melanie had ended up with the purple and Constance the red one.

Lott had taken his mask off and left it in the coach. "I have nothing to hide, and the thing's a nuisance," he'd said.

Melanie noticed that a few of the other men were also without masks, but the majority of people worn full costumes, and she found the variety and array of colors almost a blur. The crowd had already grown, and lines were forming around the food. She only selected three items on her plate, although Lott tried to help her with others.

"Not hungry?" he asked as he led her to a place at the table beside William and Constance. She shook her head. "Be sure to drink plenty of beverages, anyway. I have a feeling the halls will become stifling when the dancing starts, and you don't want to become faint."

William looked at them and smiled. His expression told Melanie, "See how well Lott takes care of you." Melanie looked away.

"I'm going to leave you with your family for a moment while I go talk with some business associates I see," Lott told her when they'd finished eating and stood from the table. "I'll come reclaim you after the dancing starts. Be sure to save the last dance for me, and I'm sure you know better than to dance with any other man more than once."

When the dancing started, no one asked Melanie to dance, but she didn't mind. The relief she felt from having some time without Lott hovering over her made her smile as the dancers floated around the floor. She sat and watched all sorts of characters and creatures dance by, William and Constance among them.

When that one ended, William asked her to dance, and she agreed. It had been so long since she'd been to something like this, she just wanted to dance.

After that, she never lacked for partners, but she made sure she didn't dance with any one of them but once. She would comply with Lott's wishes on this, because she wanted no hint of scandal.

Lott came back and they danced twice in succession. She wondered if he just wanted to stake his claim on her, because he left her again after reminding her that he would be back to claim the last dance.

The room had become suffocating and the punch hadn't helped. She sent for Gemona and stepped outside. Parts of the garden were hidden in the darkness, but lanterns illuminated the way closer to the house.

Melanie breathed in the fresher air. Gemona moved closer. "How's it going?"

"All right. At least there's been no problem, and Lott has left me alone quite a bit to talk business."

"Wonderful."

Melanie sat down on a bench, and Gemona moved away, standing where she could quickly move closer if needed. Melanie wished her friend could sit beside her and talk, but she knew how improper that would be.

"Are you tired of the party, too?"

Melanie jerked. A man sat in the shadows on another bench diagonal to hers. "No, but I needed some fresh air."

"Did you come out here alone?" His voice held such concern that she didn't feel threatened.

"No, my maid is right there." She nodded and looked in Gemona's direction. "And I'm sure Jericho is within summoning distance."

"I find it interesting that you call the slave your maid. That almost sounds like you might be from England, but I don't detect an English dialect."

She laughed. "No, I was born near here, but you do have a distinct English accent if I'm not mistaken."

"You are correct. I've been here for about four years now."

"Could you move a little closer so it would be easier to talk if we're going to carry on a conversation?" Melanie found it discerning that he remained in the shadows and she could tell little about him.

He didn't answer, but she heard movement, and suddenly he stood beside her. "May I?" He indicated the other end of the bench.

She nodded, noticing the armor costume he wore. He wore it well, but the helmet covered his face completely. She'd removed her mask and held it in her hands. Perhaps she shouldn't have.

"Are you having a good time at the ball?" He obviously searched for something to say.

"I do like to dance and I've enjoyed seeing this home, but frankly, it would have suited me to stay home."

"And why is that?"

"It's a complicated story, one I'm sure you'd rather not hear."

"I have plenty of time if you do." She could almost hear the smile in his voice. "And I'm quite sure I do want to hear it."

Melanie paused. As unreasonable as she knew it to be, she felt at ease around this man, and she found herself telling him about the suitor that became more overbearing all the time.

"You do need to extract yourself from this man," he said when she'd finished her tale.

"I know, but I haven't been able to do that with him securing my brother's support."

"Do you not have any place else to go, other relatives?"

She shook her head. "I don't."

"You are welcome to stay at my home if things become desperate. I have a housekeeper who's more like a mother, and she would welcome you with open arms."

Did he not realize the impropriety of the invitation? What an idiot she would be to show up on the doorstep of a stranger she had met briefly on a garden bench at a masquerade ball. Yet, something in his voice told her he sincerely wanted to help.

"I appreciate your kind offer, but I don't think running away is the solution. I do plan to talk with my brother when we get home, and I'm hoping that he will consider another suitor or at least more time."

"Do you know of another possible suitor?"

"There is one. He's my childhood friend and a good man, and he would treat me well."

"Do I sense some hesitation in his regard?"

She tried to see his eyes through the slit, but she could see little in the shadows and dim light. "Little escapes you, I see. Yes, I love Toby like a brother, but I don't know about having him for a husband."

They sat in a relaxed silence for a while. Melanie tried to figure out why she felt so comfortable with this man. She had no answers.

By his voice, she would guess that his age must be in the late twenties or early thirties. He stood a little taller than Lott, and he looked even stronger, yet she felt no threat at all. She turned to him. "My name is Melanie." She wouldn't give him her last name; he didn't need it.

He hesitated for what seemed like a full minute. "And I am Lucas. I like your name. I believe Melanie is an Old English name. It fits your medieval dress."

The man was not only keenly observant but also knowledgeable. "And Lucas is also unusual for an Englishman, isn't it?"

"It actually comes from Latin, but I consider myself an American now. I'm here to stay."

"I'm glad to hear it."

"And why is that?"

"I-I think our country needs all the good men it can get." She hated her stammer and hoped she didn't appear to be flirting. "Well, I guess I should return to the ballroom before someone comes searching. It's been a pleasure to talk with you, Lucas."

He stood with her. "The pleasure is all mine, Melanie. I think I will call it a night now, but may I walk you to the door before I go."

"Yes, thank you."

Someone must have propped a door open or opened more windows, because the music drifted out louder. "Might I have this dance before we part?" She heard the uncertainty in his voice, and it drew her to him.

"Yes." It came out in a whisper.

The area around the benches had been paved with bricks. He pulled her gently into his arms and began to waltz her slowly around. Melanie had never danced the new dance before, but she had no trouble following his lead.

The dance felt magical. In that moment, she could believe in Prince Charmings, gallant knights, fairy tales, and happy-ever-afters. She glided in his arms feeling more graceful and alive than she ever had in her life. She thought she liked to dance, but she hadn't really danced before now.

When the music ended, he held her a little longer, and she didn't pull away. Without a word he took her hand and placed it in the crook of his arm, but he kept his hand over hers.

Again he paused when they got to the door. "Thank you for the dance. Know that I'll be praying for you."

She watched him go. Before he rounded the corner and out of sight, he turned and waved. She waved back.

Gemona came hurrying up. "Didn't I tell you? If that wasn't a knight in shining armor, I don't know what is."

"There you are." Lott stood at the door. "I've been looking for you."

Gemona took Melanie's hidden hand and gave it a quick squeeze to say they'd talk more later.

"It became so stifling inside I stepped out to get a breath of fresh air."

"I'm afraid you missed the waltz they just played. Have you danced to a waltz before?"

"Just once."

"Are you ready to come back inside?" She realized Lott assumed she'd just come outside.

"Yes, I do believe I am." She let Gemona help her with her mask, since the maid had added ribbons to tie it on with.

"I'm told the last song will be another waltz, so I'll get to hold you in my arms then."

"I hope you'll be patient with me, since I have so little experience with waltzing."

"Of course, my dear. And I would be glad to give you some lessons when we get home."

Lott took her back inside, danced a quadrille with her, and then left her to conduct more business. Melanie could be thankful for his business interests.

She danced regularly until near midnight when Lott found her again. Everyone revealed their faces for the last dance, and Mr. Dickinson announced the winners of a costume contest Melanie knew nothing about. The winners were a jester and a mermaid that Melanie didn't know.

When Lott took her firmly in his arms for the waltz, Melanie found herself wishing for gentle arms and a kind touch that knew how to turn a dance into magic. Would she ever see Lucas again? She longed to do so with every fiber of her being, but she'd have to leave that in God's hands. She could do nothing else.

Lucas returned to the ship after leaving Melanie and went straight to his cabin. He rid himself of the armor, all the while thinking of Melanie. She didn't give him her last name, and he didn't know Miss Carter's first name, but from the story she'd told, it only made sense that they were the same person.

He fell into the chair and ran his fingers through his hair. He wanted to help her, but he didn't know how. She had rejected his offer for her to live in his home, and rightly so. He couldn't imagine why he'd made such an offer in the first place. Thankfully, she didn't appear to be offended by it, but at least she'd been using a little sense. Apparently all reason had fled him when she'd invited him to come closer.

He dared not present himself on the ship next to his in the morning the way he wanted. With his cloth mask, they'd likely shoot him for a robber; and if he didn't wear it, Melanie would run to her cabin and bolt her door once she saw his hideous scars.

But for the period they'd spent talking and dancing, for the first time ever, he'd forgotten all about his disfigured face. For a while there, he'd been the man he'd been before the accident; he'd been whole.

It must have been the fact that everyone else also wore masks, so he fit in for a change. Melanie had treated him as she would have anyone, because she didn't know he'd been maimed. If she'd known, it would have been a completely different story. That realization stabbed at his heart.

He couldn't decide if meeting Melanie had been a good or bad thing. It would make his self-imposed solitude all the harder to bear. But yet, he wouldn't wish her away if he could. She had captivated something deep within him and made his heart beat a little faster and stronger.

And she had been beautiful. He'd been able to stare at her through his armored mask without her knowing it. The lamp light danced off her red-brown hair, making it come alive. Her porcelain skin looked like rich cream, and her blue eyes were dark and royal in the dimness. He would almost believe her a figment of his imagination if he hadn't felt her in his arms.

Dancing with her had been enchanting, an almost spiritual encounter that he couldn't begin to explain. She had fit his arms so well and followed his lead so easily that she'd almost become an extension of him. Never had a dance been so special or an experience so extraordinary.

Would he ever see her again? He didn't know, but he doubted it. The loss he felt left him weak and mourning. He forced himself to get up and get ready for bed. He needed sleep to relieve his turbulent thoughts, and if God would so bless him, he might dream of dancing with a beautiful maiden in a green and gold dress.

Chapter Nine: After the Masquerade

Melanie awoke to find Gemona sitting beside her bed watching her. They had gotten back late last night or, more accurately, early this morning. She could tell the ship had already set sail by its gentle rocking, and that may have contributed to her sleeping late. The creaking of the boards may have been what woke her.

"Finally." Gemona stood. "I didn't think you would ever wake up. I'll go get you some breakfast and you can tell me all about that handsome knight while you eat."

Melanie smiled. "How could you tell how he looked when he never removed the armor which completely covered his head and face?"

"'Handsome is as handsome does,' and I saw how he treated you with great respect." Gemona gave her a smug look. "Another man we know should take lessons." With that, Gemona left the room, and Melanie snuggled back down in bed.

She let her mind drift back to the conversation with Lucas and how special it made her feel to have someone truly interested in what she had to say. She'd not had that on a regular basis since her father had passed away. William stayed busy and tolerated her interruptions, but he had become more involved in his own affairs. Constance only became interested when they discussed fashion or made purchases, but even then she only listened when Melanie agreed with her. And Lott's attention focused on making sure she did what he wanted.

She relived again how it felt to be held so tenderly and be lead in the most enchanted dance of her life. She floated in his arms without touching the ground, and during that dance, they'd forged some kind of special connection, a bond that she couldn't explain. Had he felt it, too?

Despite how irrational it might be, she wanted to believe that they might meet another time. Why would they have such a strong, instant connection only to never see each other again?

Gemona came in carrying a tray. Melanie slipped out of bed, put on her wrapper, and sat down at the tiny table anchored to the wall.

Gemona couldn't wait to hear Melanie's account of Lucas, so she told her story. She tried to just stick with what had happened and leave the emotion from her voice, but Gemona knew her too well.

"You like him?" her maid asked with a satisfied smile when Melanie had finished.

She saw no use in denying it, so she nodded. "But I doubt if our paths will ever meet again."

"You don't know that. It would have been easier if you'd gotten his last name, but there can't be that many men around with the name Lucas."

"I don't know. There were people at the ball from a wide area."

"Yes, but we only have to look among the rich, because no other people attended the ball, and that narrows it down considerably."

"How will I go about finding him? I can't exactly ask for William's help."

"You just leave that up to me. I have my ways."

Melanie didn't doubt that. Gemona was one of the most resourceful persons she'd ever seen.

They returned home, and things returned to the usual routine. At first, Melanie and Gemona discussed Lucas and the ball every night. However, as the days passed without Gemona being able to find even a grain of information about him, he eventually receded into the background, but that didn't mean he faded from Melanie's thoughts. Sir Lucas stayed with her wherever she went, and she knew he visited her dreams, although she couldn't always remember them clearly.

Although Lott didn't come to visit as often as he once had, he became more insistent that Melanie marry him. Two days after they returned home, he'd dropped to his knees in the garden and asked her to become his wife. She had begged for more time, but she knew the sand in the hourglass had about sifted down, and she wouldn't be able to stall for much longer. Lott was not a patient man.

She went to talk with William, despite the fact that he'd been hard at work since returning from Edenton. "Lott has asked me to marry him."

"I heard. But Jenkins said you put him off."

She didn't like the fact that Lott had already told William and likely only his side of things. "I did, and I'm not sure I can marry him."

"Of course you can marry him! What nonsense!" William's outburst surprised her and gave her a sinking feeling, but she sailed ahead.

"I came to ask you to consider Toby. He's always been a good friend, and I think we would deal well together. He has an easier personality than Lott."

"Has Askew proposed?"

"No. Of course not or I would have told you, but I feel certain he would if given the opportunity and the least hint that I might accept."

"You need to think about this, Mel. Askew might be a nice enough guy, but he's not for you. The Askews are good people, but they don't have the financial resources to give you the life you're accustomed to. Why you wouldn't know how to cook him a meal, do his laundry, or perform any of the other household chores he'd require. The Askews have a couple of field hands, but they can't afford house slaves."

Melanie looked down at her hands. She hadn't thought of the fact that she might not make Toby an adequate wife.

"I'm disappointed in you," William continued. "All this time, I've been telling Jenkins that Askew is nothing more than a childhood friend, and here I find out that he is more. You've made a liar out of me, and you've lied to me as well."

Her head jerked up and her eyes widened. "No, William. He is nothing more than a childhood friend, but even that is more tolerable than a cruel man who will deal with me so harshly. I fear for my wellbeing if I marry Lott."

"What blarney! I can't understand why you're acting so foolish about this. Maybe Lott is right and we've spoiled you. I guess I should have been stricter on you, and I know father should have. He doted on you, and that's part of your problem."

"And I don't understand why Lott wants to marry someone who finds him repugnant."

William banged his fist on his desk. "Enough! I will have no more of this. Just be glad that Lott does want you, because he can provide for you more lavishly than even you are accustomed."

Melanie stood knowing that her efforts had been in vain. "There's more to life than wealth, William, and you need to remember that. And if Lott maims or kills me in a fit of rage, it will be upon your head."

"You should think about not bringing him to that point of fury, because right now, I know exactly how he might feel."

Melanie left the room quickly without saying another word. She'd said too much already, and she didn't want William to see the tears forming in her eyes and think her a weak, weepy female. But his betrayal drove a knife deep into her heart.

"Well, it's apparent that we'll have to take matters into our own hands." Gemona paced the floor, seemingly too anxious to sit down, after Melanie told the maid about her meeting with William.

"What can we do?"

"I think it's time to consider eloping with Toby."

Melanie hung her head. "I can't."

Gemona stopped her pacing and stared. "Why ever not?"

William just pointed out that I'm not a fit wife for Toby. I don't know how to cook or clean or do any of the tasks the wife of a farmer should be able to do."

"Then you'll learn, and Toby already knows that about you and yet he still wants to marry you anyway. Love can conquer anything, and that man loves you."

"But I don't love him – not in that way. Toby deserves so much more. He deserves a wife who will cherish and love him in a romantic way, too. It would be awfully selfish of me to marry him when I will never be that woman. I can't do that to my best friend."

"Even though you would make him the happiest man on earth."

"But for how long? I know he would be ecstatic to start with, but when do you think he'd start realizing my heart wasn't in our union? When would he start feeling cheated?"

Gemona shook her head. "You're a better woman than you know. Half of you might just be enough for Toby."

"Might? You want me to marry on a 'might?' I'd rather live in misery with Lott than to make Toby miserable. No, I can't marry Toby Askew. I wish I could. I wish I could love him the way he deserves to be loved."

"You could learn to love him." They both recognized the statement as Gemona's last poor attempt to win her argument, and Melanie didn't bother to answer.

Sunday afternoon Lott sat in the parlor with the family, and he turned to Melanie. "If you don't agree to marry me and set a date, William has agreed to have the announcement made and I'll set the date for us."

Her eyes flew to William. He nodded, his face hard and unmoving.

She felt caught in a cruel trap from which there'd be no escape, and she knew the sand had just all run down. The best she could hope for would be to postpone the wedding for as long as possible. She sighed. "All right. I will marry you."

Lott's face gleamed with the pride of a victor. "When? I wanted to have my bride by winter, but here it is November already."

"With Christmas approaching and wedding plans and arrangements to make, I can't see how we could possibly be married before spring."

"That's too long to wait. I'm tired of spending cold winter nights alone."

Melanie couldn't believe he'd made that comment in front of Constance and William. She looked at her brother, but he didn't appear to think anything amiss.

"She's quite right." Her support came from Constance, of all people. "This must be the wedding people will talk about for years, and you can't plan that in a fortnight. We'll have to have Melanie's dress made, and the fabric or trims may have to be ordered from Europe. Invitations will need to be printed and sent out. It would be lovely to have some flowers in the church, and those won't be available until around May. In fact, I think spring might be pushing things."

For the first time ever, Melanie could be thankful for Constance's worldly values. She looked for Lott's reaction. *Oh, Lord, please let him agree to the delay.*

"If you wait too late, we'll be uncomfortably hot in our finery."

Constance nodded. "Shall we say late May, then?"

"Or early June," Melanie added, knowing she wouldn't be able to ask for any later.

"Early June it is." William made the final decision. "Most of the crops should be in the ground at the plantation by then."

Setting the wedding date had put Lott into a good mood. "Get your wraps and come outside with me. We won't stay long, but the sun is out, and the day doesn't feel too cold."

She collected her wool cape, gloves, and Gemona, and followed Lott outside. The garden looked bare, but he found a spot that couldn't be seen from the house.

"Thank you for finally agreeing to be my wife." He kept his voice low and seductive. She knew he planned to kiss her even before he started lowering his head. "Not even your slave can object to me kissing my fiancée."

His thin lips felt cold and hard, and she felt like gagging when his tongue probed her mouth. To escape, her thoughts ran to Lucas, and she wished with all her might that he'd kissed her that night in Edenton after they'd danced. She didn't want her first kiss to be from Lott and to be so disgusting. How would she manage if she did have to marry him?

Gemona just shook her head when they got back to Melanie's room. "Dealing with that man's like trying to handle the devil, but at least we have a few months. Anything might happen between now and then."

Melanie needed Gemona's optimism. "That's what I'm hoping and praying for, too."

Constance said they needed to hold an engagement party, and Lott wanted to hold it at his place. However, he wanted Melanie and Constance to plan and organize everything. "Spare no expense he told them. I want it to be impressive just like I will the wedding."

Constance threw herself into the preparations with an exuberance Melanie had never seen before, and Melanie gladly let her sister-in-law take over. She just didn't care.

Lucas went home with an uneasiness he couldn't quiet define, but he knew it had to do with Melanie's situation and his inability to help her. Every action he could think of would not be well-received, and his scarred face prevented some of them.

He understood that Melanie had only been congenial because she knew nothing of his disfigurement, but he wanted to help her out of her dilemma, even if he repulsed her. Because of her, his life had suddenly shifted; and he didn't know if it would be for better or worse. At least, concern for her had sent him to his knees in prayer, and he felt sure his renewed relationship with God would be good.

Glenna met him as soon as he walked in the house. "How did it go?"

"All right, I guess."

"How long did you stay at the ball?"

"At least five hours."

She grinned. "You must have had a good time then."

"I did rather enjoy some of it." He couldn't deny how much he had enjoyed meeting Melanie.

"Did you dance at all?"

"Yes. Once."

"Did you meet anyone special?"

"Enough with all the questions. I went to the ball, stayed for hours, even danced, and therefore paid my debt. Now I'd like a little peace and quiet. How did things go here in my absence?"

"Things went just fine here, but don't think you'll divert me from what we're discussing." Her Irish eyes twinkled in amusement. "There's only one reason that you wouldn't want to tell me about the masquerade, and I will discover who she is eventually."

He ignored the intuitive woman and proceeded to his suite.

Lucas rode like the wind across the meadow and went fishing often to take advantage of the autumn weather before winter arrived, but Melanie went with him. She might recede into the background at times, depending on the events, but thoughts of her never strayed far.

He tried to tell himself it was due to the isolated way he lived and the loneliness that often surrounded him. He didn't believe in falling in love the first time two people met. Actually, he didn't even know if he believed in love at all. Two weeks ago he would have said a vehement "no," but now he didn't know quite how he felt. Now he felt uncertain about everything.

If life played out on a stage, he'd been placed on a revolving one, and the entire scene had just completely changed in the blink of an eye. But he knew his play must be a tragedy. How could it be anything else? His hand absently felt for the rough ridges on the right side of his face.

However, meeting Melanie hadn't been the only life-changing event to come from his trip to Edenton. He'd also renewed his relationship with God. Now he didn't feel as abandoned and alone as he had. Yet, indirectly, Melanie had been responsible for that momentous event, too. He'd let go of some of his resentment and bitterness and prayed to God on her behalf. He'd been praying ever since.

On a blustery day in mid-November, he decided to tell Glenna about turning back to God. She barely let him get his story told.

"Oh, Lucas! That does this old heart good." Her hands flew to her chest, as if she wanted to hold her runaway heart in check. "I've been praying for this day ever since you became so bitter. What caused the change?"

He should have anticipated that question. He breathed in all the air his lungs would hold and let it out slowly. Still, he sat there in silence for a while longer. But Glenna could be patient when the situation warranted it.

 He decided he'd kept Melanie to himself long enough. How many times had he turned their short time together over in his mind to enjoy every facet of it? How many hours had he spent in trying to come up with a way to help her situation? But now he wanted to hear someone else's opinion and advice. No one would be better than Glenna at giving either.

Surprisingly, his housekeeper sat quietly and listened while he recounted what had happened in the garden on the night of the ball. He didn't mention anything about his feelings, but he didn't have to. The woman knew him too well.

"It thrills me no end to see your interests turn to someone else for a change."

Did Glenna think he'd grown too selfish? He took a moment to reflect on that. She could be right. The accident had turned him outside in.

Then she began to ask her many questions. "What kind of costume did Melanie wear? Did he get to see what she looked like? Was she pretty? Did she talk about her family? Where did she live?"

He answered them all as truthfully as he could. She'd dressed as a lady from the Middle Ages. She had a small mask that covered the area around her eyes, but she'd taken it off when he met her in the garden. She had dark blue eyes and long hair, more red than brown, which she'd worn in a plait down her back; and, yes, she had been very pretty. She didn't say much about her family, but she did have an older, married brother. He didn't know where she lived.

When he backed up and told Glenna about hearing the argument between Jenkins and Melanie on the ship the night before and her brother's reaction, she gasped. Concern crinkled her brow.

"The problem is, I don't know what to do to help her, but I feel as if I need to do something. My heart goes out to her predicament."

"And to her, I'd be thinking."

He didn't bother to deny it. "The only thing I can think of is to hire a detective to track her down, but unless he could do something that might improve her situation, I'm not sure it would help. This scarred body of mine prevents me from being able to directly help."

Glenna looked pensive. "But having an investigator delve into her personal life in such an underhanded way doesn't sit right with me. It almost feels criminal."

"I've thought of that, too. I wouldn't like it if someone investigated me without my knowledge, and the Bible clearly states that we are to treat others as we'd want them to treat us."

She smiled. "It's so good to hear you referring to the Bible. But there's no reason why you couldn't go and talk with her if you can find where she lives. I could ask around for you."

He snorted. "There's every reason. I'm sure I wouldn't be well-received by anyone, including Melanie. She has one monster in her life, and she has no need of another."

Glenna stiffened. "Don't you dare compare yourself to that bully, Jenkins. By what you've said, Melanie enjoyed her time with you. She'd probably love to see you again."

"She thinks I'm a whole man, though. She doesn't know how hideous I look now. I can guarantee you I would have never had that dance or the conversation with her if I hadn't had my face covered."

"You don't know that, and I don't think you're giving the girl enough credit. Not everyone is as materialistic and self-centered as Margaret Ann."

"That's a nice thought, Glenna, and I wish it were true, but you and I both know better." Even he could hear the bitterness and regret in his voice. "I saw people divert their eyes in disgust over and over again before I decided to keep the scars hidden."

Glenna stood as if about to give a lecture. "I know no such thing." She leaned closer. "How can you be sure you're not wrong when you never give anyone a chance? I've never turned from you, and your scars only bother me to the extent of how they've changed you. The hurts you've let scar you on the inside are much worse than the physical ones on the outside. Although there's not much you can do for the ones on the outside, you can heal on the inside. It's your choice not to."

She stopped just for a moment to gain her breath and then continued. "You asked for my opinion, and there you have it. As for my advice, since you are so thick-skulled and won't consider going to her, then turn the matter over to God. Let Him take care of things. In fact, that's probably the very best solution of all. My only fear is that God wants to use you, that he'll tell you to act, and you won't listen to him, just like you don't listen to me." With that, she turned and walked out.

Lucas leaned back in his chair and closed his eyes. The perfect image of Melanie rose before him, as clearly as if she stood there in person. Why would a lovely woman like her want anything to do with someone like him? She wouldn't. Glenna was wrong about this. Her maternal love for him had clouded her reasoning.

Chapter Ten: Christmas

Constance's plans for the engagement party had been going well, but they came to a near standstill with the approach of Christmas. Everything would be put on hold until after the holidays, which suited Melanie fine. In fact, nothing would have pleased her more than dispensing with the wedding and anything to do with it forever, but that wouldn't happen.

Gemona still argued with her about Toby. "I'll go with you and teach you everything you need to know about keeping house for him, if that's what's worrying you. Or is it that you don't want to learn and have to do such laborious tasks for the rest of your life?"

Melanie couldn't believe Gemona had even suggested that. "Surely you know me better than that. If I loved Toby romantically, I would be glad to have you teach me such things, but I don't. Toby deserves someone who can love him as a wife should. I never will; I wish I could. Besides, as a lady's maid, are you sure you know enough to teach me household tasks?"

Gemona ignored the question. "So you're going to live with an evil man who will make your life miserable so that Toby might find a woman who will love him more than you?"

Melanie raised her chin and felt her body stiffen in resolve. "Yes."

"What makes you think that will ever happen? What if you are the only woman he will ever love, and he'd be happier with you than alone or with anyone else?"

Melanie paused. She hadn't thought of that. "God hasn't given me peace about marrying Toby."

Gemona huffed. "And He's given you peace about marrying Lott?"

"No. Of course not. But I'm praying that something will happen, and I won't have to."

"I don't know why I even bother trying to talk any sense into you. You can be one stubborn woman, and that may just be your downfall; because, if you marry Lott Jenkins, you will live to regret it. It won't take a year before you'll be wishing you'd eloped with Toby instead of marrying such a man."

Tears formed in Melanie's eyes despite her best effort to stop them. "I'm just trying to do the best I can, given the situation I find myself in. The way I see it, I can be miserable, or both Toby and I can be miserable."

Gemona's face softened, and she pulled Melanie into a comforting hug. "Oh, honey. I don't know why you think you'd make Toby miserable. I'm sure you'd make him one very happy man, and loving him like a best friend is more than most women offer, but I didn't mean to upset you so. I just want what's best for you, and I know that's not Lott Jenkins."

Melanie nodded and let Gemona's pats on the back comfort her. "I know."

A few days later, Gemona tried a different tactic. "Toby wants to talk with you. He'll pick us up after your ladies' society meeting this week."

"I'm not going to meet Toby. I'm engaged to be married now, and I will not meet with another man on the sly regardless of who the man is."

"Why are you being so mulish about this?"

"I'm just trying to do what's right. If not immoral, it's certainly unethical for me to be slipping around behind my fiancé's back to see another man, even if there's nothing going on. It would definitely give the impression of impropriety."

Gemona sighed her resignation. "Well, will you at least let him write to you?"

"Only if he writes as an old friend and mentions nothing of us getting together in any other way."

"All right." Gemona didn't seem as disappointed as Melanie expected. "I'll let Toby know."

The following morning, Melanie awoke with a smile on her face. She'd had the most wonderful dream. At first, she had been dancing on a large brick patio with

Lucas. Then they were transported to the sky where they danced on clouds, and his arms felt even better than they had the first time. When he whisked her off to ride a magnificent horse beside his, she felt the wind against her face, and Lucas flashed her his happy smile, she wanted to stay with him for the rest of her life. Her dream ended with a kiss, one warm and inviting and filled with passion and love – one different in every way from the kiss Lott had given her.

Lott hadn't had the opportunity to kiss her again, but she knew he'd demand one somehow after their engagement had been announced. She did not relish the idea.

Melanie got the idea Lucas visited her dreams much more than she could recall the next morning. However, she did remember several, and she tucked them away along with her memories of their time in the garden in Edenton to bring out and cherish when she needed some happiness to hold onto.

The two weeks before Christmas became busy indeed. It had become a tradition for the wealthier families to visit among each other just prior to Christmas Eve, which fell on a Thursday this year. The invitations varied, ranging from dropping in for refreshments and conversation, to parties, to dinners. Sometimes, they even attended affairs in Murfreesboro or Colerain.

Melanie usually enjoyed the events, but this year Lott attended many with them, and that added extra stress. Even at his best, she couldn't be herself around him.

Everywhere she went, she looked for Lucas, but she had been disappointed so far. She felt sure he must fit into their circle of friends and acquaintances, since he'd attended the masquerade ball. Perhaps he lived to the south of Edenton and too far from her. She'd discretely tried to learn if anyone knew of him, and Gemona had asked among the slaves, too, but no one seemed to know anything. Her knight remained a mystery.

They received an invitation from the Askews to come to supper on Wednesday evening before Christmas. Melanie smiled, because she felt reasonably sure Lott would not be invited.

"I see no need in attending," Constance told William. "We've had plenty of other events to attend."

"Do we have another engagement on Wednesday?" William asked.

"Well, no, but it would be nice to spend an evening at home, since we've had something every night this week."

"That's what tomorrow and Friday are for." William gave his wife a hard look. "The Askews have been closer friends than most over the years, especially when my parents were alive. I think we should go. It would slight them if we didn't."

"Very well." Constance had learned when William would not be swayed.

However, when Wednesday afternoon came, Constance had developed a headache and queasy stomach. Melanie wondered if she just didn't want to go to the Askews'. By the look William gave his wife, he must have thought the same thing, but he said nothing.

"You give Toby serious consideration," Gemona told her as she helped her dress. "Looks like he's the only other option you're going to have."

Gemona hadn't accompanied Melanie to most of the affairs, since she had attended with her family, and they could act as chaperones. The maid wouldn't go tonight, either.

Melanie climbed into the carriage feeling lighter than she had in weeks. Not only would she be free of Lott tonight, but William wouldn't be nearly as observant as Constance would have been, and she'd get to see her best friend. *Thank you, Lord.*

"What would you like from me for a wedding present, Mel? Since Lott is taking care of the wedding expenses, even your trousseau, I want to give you something. Of course, I am giving Lott a sizable dowry, but I will recoup that soon enough. He's already told me I won't have to pay him to find a buyer for my harvests and get them to market, and he'll get me better prices than I could get."

Melanie caught herself from saying she felt as if William had sold her to Lott. "Gemona. I would like for you to put Gemona specifically in my name."

"Lott is going to consider your property his."

"I know, but you asked me what I wanted. On the second thought, set her free. That way she can make the decision where she wants to be."

"Are you sure? She might not want to stay with you, and it makes more sense to me to put her in your name if she's to be a gift."

"I'm sure." This way Gemona could leave if Lott abused her, and Melanie knew neither liked the other very much, but she dare not tell William. For some reason, neither he nor Constance wished to hear anything negative against Lott.

The joy on Toby's face when she walked into the parlor nearly took her breath. In fact the whole family seemed happy to see her. William sat next to Mr. Askew, and the two of them began talking about farming.

Melanie handed Mrs. Askew the package of cookies Constance had sent, and she knew the older woman would send some baked goods back with her. It had become one of their traditions.

She and Toby settled into a corner of the parlor to exchange gifts. They were the only ones to do this, but they had done so since they were children.

She had bought him a pocket watch with his name engraved in it. He gave her a gold chain with a cross, anchor, and heart pendants on it. Faith, hope, and charity, she caught its message right away. How appropriate considering her situation.

"I'll treasure it," she told him. "You always choose the best gifts."

"I'll treasure my watch, too," and his eyes told her just how much.

Mrs. Askew drew Melanie into the kitchen "I have everything just about done," the older woman said. "Would you mind helping me set the food on the sideboard?"

Melanie could handle that. As she followed Mrs. Askew with the last item, a gravy boat, she thought aloud. "I wish I knew how to cook. I'm afraid I would make a poor wife for someone who didn't have house servants."

Mrs. Askew stopped and looked at Melanie. "If you want to marry such a man, don't let your inexperience in household tasks stop you. You just come to me, and I'll teach you what you need to know."

Did Mrs. Askew know that Toby would like to marry her? Melanie couldn't tell from her expression, but she would guess she did. Didn't a mother often know her son's heart?

Just as she put the last dish in place, Toby wandered in. "I thought you might need some help."

Mrs. Askew gave her son an amused look. "We're ready. Go call your father and Mr. Carter to the table."

"Where are your other sons tonight?" William asked.

"Well, you know, the three oldest are married with places of their own, and they couldn't come tonight for one reason or another. The next two are courting tonight, and that just leaves Toby here."

"We're so glad you came, though," Mrs. Askew added. "It would be pitiful with just the three of us. I'm just sorry your wife didn't feel well and hope she'll be fine by tomorrow."

"Thank you. I do, too." William looked over at Mr. Askew. "I don't know if you've heard or not, but Melanie …"

"I've been looking forward to seeing you so much I could hardly wait." Melanie cut him off in mid-sentence, sure that he had been about to announce her engagement, and she feared that announcement would make the Askews uncomfortable. In addition, Lott wouldn't want the Askews at the engagement party, and she didn't want their feelings hurt. She did plan to invite them to the wedding, however.

"That's right. Coming here has been all she's talked about for days." William must have caught on to his near faux pas.

"Well, we're so glad to have you." Mrs. Askew looked pleased.

As the conversation continued in niceties, Melanie looked around her. The Askews were in no way poor the way Constance often made them out to be. Their two-

story, framed farmhouse looked very comfortable. They
were much better off than many of the others in the area.

She noticed Toby watching her, and he smiled
when their eyes met. At least, he didn't appear
uncomfortable around her, and she sensed no
awkwardness between them. His friendship had always
been a blessing, and she thanked God that hadn't
changed by her refusal to elope with him. She smiled
back.

William followed Mr. Askew back into the parlor
after the meal. Their conversation had turned from
farming to politics, and it had William's full attention.

Melanie stood and turned to Mrs. Askew. "If you
will get things set up, I'll wash the dishes." She had
observed that task enough she felt sure she could handle
it.

"No." Mrs. Askew shook her head. "You're our
guest. Go on into the parlor, and I'll join you in a few
minutes. This won't take me long."

Melanie set a hurt look on her face. "I thought of
myself as more to this family than just a visitor."

Mrs. Askew paused, considering what Melanie had
said. "You are, but you'll need some help."

"I'll help her." Toby's offer came at once.

Mrs. Askew looked torn, but the young people
won out. "All right, then. I'll be in the parlor with the
men."

Toby prepared a pan of soapy water for the wash
and one with plain water for the rinse, and Melanie set

about washing. She didn't have much to do since Toby brought her the dishes in the order they should be washed, took them out of the rinse water, and dried them.

"This is the first time I've ever washed dishes." She wanted him to know her inexperience in household chores.

"I always knew you were a fast learner. Do you remember how I often struggled to keep up with you in the schoolroom?" She and the two youngest Askew boys had shared a tutor for a while.

"That's not how I remember it. You challenged me and often kept me studying well into the night to keep up with you."

He chuckled. "Then I guess we did that for each other."

She sighed. "Those were good times. Sometimes I wish I could go back and live them again. Things were certainly simpler then."

"I know you don't want any declarations from me, but let me just say that any offers I have made in the past are still good. And, if you ever need me for any reason, just let me know. No matter what else happens, we will always be best of friends."

She put her hand over one of his mindful not to get soapy water on his shirt. "Thank you. It means the world to me to know that."

His eyes told her all the things she'd told him not to say, and she looked away with tears in her eyes. *Lord, am I doing the right thing in not eloping with this man? Marrying him would make things so much easier for me than marrying Lott, but I want to do what's best for all of us, not just me. Guide me, Lord. Help me to know Thy will, I pray.*

"Don't be sad, Mellie. I don't understand why you would marry Lott instead of me, but it doesn't change my regard for you."

"I've been given no choice in the matter."

"It's not like you to be so compliant on something this important." He put up his hands when he saw her start to protest at the path this conversation had taken. "All right. I'm hushing. Just write and let me know what's happening with you. Tell me your thoughts like you used to. I'm worried about you."

She tried to smile but imagined it looked pretty weak. "I am, too, but I'm counting on God's intervention."

"Just remember that God often sends others to help instead of changing the situation."

Had God sent Gemona and Toby to rescue her, and her refusal went against His will? Deep down she clung to the belief that God wanted her to marry a man she loved and loved her back. Marriage shouldn't be one-sided. Oh, she knew many had marriages arranged by their families, and more than a few came to love each other eventually, but, in her mind, that went about it all backwards. It made more sense to her to find the love first. Had she been reading too many of those romance novels?

Toby must have seen how reflective she'd become. "I don't want to put added pressure on you or make things harder in any way. If I can only have you as a friend, then I'll accept that. What I can't accept is losing you, and if you marry Jenkins, I'm afraid I'll lose you one way or another. I doubt he will approve of our friendship."

"I don't want to talk about it any longer. Why spoil our time together with something we have no answers for right now. Let's enjoy each other's company, because it may be a long time before we ever have another opportunity."

Somehow her comment made him happy, and a wide grin spread across his face. "You're right. I'm so glad you came tonight and that you talk to me like always. I feared you might be hesitant to be around me or awkward in my presence."

She nudged his arm with her shoulder. "Never. We'll always be close, even if we never saw each other again."

His eyes told her how much joy he found in her words. But they also spoke to her of love, and she turned from him. "We're finished. Shall we join the others?"

He hung his towel on a peg. "If we must. I guess we should before William realizes we've been in the kitchen together, and we find ourselves in trouble."

She laughed, trying to lighten the mood. "It wouldn't be the first time we got in trouble now, would it?"

He laughed, too. "Indeed, it wouldn't."

Melanie enjoyed Christmas Eve. Jericho had gone hunting and came back with a turkey and some squirrels. They would go to Lott's tomorrow for Christmas dinner, so they used tonight for a family time of a roasted turkey dinner, carols, and opening presents. Perhaps the moment held more meaning for Melanie, because something told her this would be the last time it would be just the three of them. The presents were the usual ones of books, clothing, or jewelry, but the sense of family meant more than anything. She was glad those closest to her had chosen to give Christmas gifts, Most people didn't, but Melanie liked the giving.

Despite their recent conflicts, William had become her guardian and given her a home after their parents died, and she would always be grateful. She knew he had convinced himself that Lott would be her best choice in a husband. She just wished he could see how wrong he was.

William cleared his throat. "We have an announcement to make. Constance is in a family way, and you'll be an aunt sometime around June or July. Now we know why Constance hasn't been feeling her best recently."

Melanie jumped up and hugged Constance and then William. "I'm so happy for you."

"I may not be able to attend your wedding, since my time will be near and I'll be big by then, but we'll have everything ready ahead of time."

Thoughts of the wedding dampened some of Melanie's joy. "I'm sure you're right. You have so many of the plans in place already."

The weather on Christmas Day turned cold and blustery. Heavy clouds hung in the sky, and Melanie wondered if the wind would blow in snow. For now, the day just looked drab and dismal, but it suited her mood as they made their way to Lott's.

Constance had been feeling poorly this morning, but she ate a little toast, had some tea, and declared she thought the sickness would wear off with some fresh air. So William helped them into the carriage, put heated bricks at their feet, and bundled them in blankets and rugs for their trip to Lott's.

When they arrived, they made their way to the door while Jericho took the carriage around to the back. The slave would take Melanie's present for Lott and give it to the butler to be presented later if Lott gave her one.

Lott came to meet them in the hall not long after the butler opened the door. "It's so good to see you." He gave Melanie a kiss on the cheek and took her hand to lead her into the parlor. "Come. Let's talk while the slaves put the finishing touches on our dinner. We have a ham big enough to feed an army."

"It smells delicious," Melanie said, because she knew he expected some comment from her. However, she saw Constance wrinkle her nose as if she found the smells coming from the kitchen intolerable.

"Yes, they're cooking in the house today with the weather looking precarious. We sometimes do that, although we have a summer kitchen for when hotter weather arrives."

Melanie nodded, and he continued. "When we marry, you can take charge and have things to suit you. I don't care how it's done as long as everything runs smoothly."

The housekeeper soon called them to dinner, and they spent a long time in leisurely eating and pleasant talk. Lott had become much more agreeable since she had agreed to marry him, and Melanie hoped that proved to be a good sign. However, she still hoped of a miracle that would extract her from the situation.

"This has been wonderful," Constance told Lott as they made their way back to the parlor, although Melanie had noticed her sister-in-law only ate a little of the food and none of the ham.

"Do you play the piano?" Lott asked Melanie.

"Only a little. Constance plays better than I do."

He turned to Constance. "Would you play so we can sing along?"

She did, and the rest of them stood around the piano and sang. Lott's tenor voice tended to wander off-key, but he sang low and unobtrusively, so unlike the man in general.

He put his arm around Melanie's waist as they sang, and she stiffened to keep herself from stepping away from him. "You have an angelic voice," Lott whispered in her ear.

When they tired of standing, they moved from the piano and took seats. Lott made sure he maneuvered Melanie to sit beside him on the small settee. "If you'd like to resume music lessons after we marry, just let me know. I'm open to you pursuing any such interests. And if you want to redecorate the house, we can do that, too."

Melanie looked around at the lavish furnishings, which didn't appeal to her tastes. She wouldn't know where to begin.

"You might want to leave these rooms as they are for entertaining and start with your suite."

She wondered if he and she would have separate bedrooms, but now wouldn't be the time to ask. Regardless, she knew without a doubt Lott would expect her to be available whenever he wanted her.

With William's permission, Lott took her into the library when time drew near for them to leave. He handed her a beautiful, hand-painted jewelry box. The black, lacquered box had red and pink roses in different stages of growth painted all over it.

"This is lovely."

He looked pleased. "I plan to fill it for you."

She got up and went to the door to call for the butler to bring his present. Jericho had seen that it got into the servant's hands after he dropped them off at the front door.

Lott looked pleased with the wooden humidor, hand-carved with intricate designs. "So we both gave each other wooden boxes. I find that a good sign, and thank you."

He took her in his arms, as she knew he would. "Now for the best present of all."

His mouth devoured hers, and she tried not to show how much she hated the kiss. She wished he'd at least be gentle.

"You are so sweet." Apparently he hadn't noticed anything amiss. He rested his forehead on hers for a few moments after he ended the kiss. "I can't wait for June to get here."

Although the day hadn't been altogether bad, Melanie rode home glad that it had ended. Now if she could just have sweet dreams of a handsome knight instead of nightmares of Lott.

Chapter Eleven: The Engagement Party

Constance and William decided to hold a New Year's party. Melanie saw it as an unnecessary expense, but as usual, her opinion held little weight. William appeared to rely on Lott's help after she married him, and that caused him to be less tight-fisted with his money. They'd invite a number of their friends and acquaintances, and William wanted to include the Askews.

Constance didn't agree. "With the adverse reaction Lott Jenkins had to Toby, I don't think that's a good idea."

"They're our friends, and I can't see not inviting them. Of all the people I know, the Askews are the ones most likely to help out if we needed it."

"I think Lott will replace them soon in that regard." Constance looked at Melanie.

"Nonetheless, I can't slight the Askews like this. A man can have more than one good friend."

"Well, if you insist." Constance still didn't look happy. "But if there's trouble, it will be on your head."

William looked at Melanie. "What do you think, Mel?"

"If there's trouble, it won't come from the Askews." She dare not say Lott would be the troublemaker, but they would know her meaning. "And I agree with you, William. The Askews would be very hurt to learn we had a party for our friends and didn't invite them. They've been too loyal over the years to be treated that way."

He nodded, dismissing the question as answered. Constance gave in as she usually did when William became adamant.

With Constance being indisposed long into the morning on most days, most of the arrangements fell on Melanie. Constance made the plans and gave them to Melanie to carry out. She enjoyed taking care of the decorations where she could make the decisions, but she would have made different choices as far as the food and other areas went.

A cold rain fell on December thirty-first. It started off as little more than a mist, but as the day progressed, it became heavier.

"This will put a real damper on everything," Constance complained.

"It may cut down on attendance," William agreed, "but I think you invited more than the house would hold if everyone came."

"I'll need to pull in some extra staff to take care of the mud tracked in."

"Do whatever you need, dear." William sounded ready to dismiss the conversation. "If you need me to bring a couple of slaves from the plantation to work in the stables, we can take some of the better stable hands and bring them to the front of the house. Jericho is capable in any position you place him in."

Constance nodded and went to talk with the cook. Melanie needed to get up and help, but she'd tired of so many social affairs. There'd been no time to rest since September, when preparations were in full-swing to go to the masquerade ball. With her accepting Lott's proposal, everything had gotten busier, and Christmas just added more activity and confusion. Now they were entertaining to bring in the New Year, and the engagement party would follow in February.

She forced herself to get moving. Maybe staying busy would keep her mind from her impending marriage. Would there even be time to relax between the engagement party and wedding? With Constance's plans, she doubted it.

Lott arrived first, and Melanie wondered if he came early hoping to get her alone. She'd try to make sure that didn't happen. However, she had little hope of avoiding his kiss at midnight.

Mrs. Askew and Toby arrived next. "My husband sends his regrets, but he's come down with a nasty cold and decided to stay in this evening."

"It is a messy, cold rain out there." Melanie accepted her hug.

Lott's face turned red when he spied Toby, but William introduced everyone, seemingly unaware of the tension. Toby handled the situation better. He extended his hand, and Lott finally took it, although stiffly.

"It's so good of you to invite us." Mrs. Askew smiled warmly at William. "We enjoyed having you over for dinner so much before Christmas, it's good to see you again so soon. We don't get together nearly often enough anymore."

Lott looked ready to explode. "You went to their house before Christmas?" He directed the question toward Melanie.

"William and I did. Constance didn't feel well enough to go that day."

He glared at William. "Why wasn't I informed about this?"

"I didn't know you needed to be." William looked truly perplexed.

"Melanie is my fiancée, and I don't want her visiting other men."

William frowned. "The Askews are long-time friends. Melanie visited with the family and not just Toby. Besides, she went with me, and I assure you she behaved properly."

Thankfully, the Askews remained silent during this exchange, although Mrs. Askew looked stunned. Was she shocked at Lott's unreasonable remarks or at the fact that Melanie had agreed to marry him? Probably some of both. Gemona must have told Toby about her engagement, but since the announcement wouldn't be made until the engagement party, Mrs. Ashew likely didn't know. Melanie didn't think Toby would want to be the bearer of that news. No, he'd rather forget about it altogether.

At first, if Lott didn't stay right beside her, he watched her closely. However, as more people arrived, and her task of helping Constance oversee everything pulled her away, he started talking with some of the men.

"Jenkins is just as bad as Gemona told me." Toby caught her in the kitchen. "I hoped she'd exaggerated. You can't marry him, Mellie. You just can't."

"I don't want to." She kept her voice down to a whisper. Although the slaves would never say anything that would cause her problems, she didn't want to take the chance of anyone else hearing. "I keep praying for a miracle."

"Where's your sister?" She heard Lott ask William, and he sounded closer.

Toby exited through the back entrance. Thankfully, he knew the house well. Melanie went out to return to the guests.

"There you are." Lott frowned at her. "Where have you been?"

"I just went to the kitchen to check on some things for Constance." They weren't serving supper, but the refreshments were extensive, and Constance had a tendency for extravagance. Perhaps that contributed to the estate's financial problems.

"Then, come along dear." He looked behind her to see if he could see anyone before turning and leading her toward the parlor. "The dancing is about to start, and I want to dance the first one with you."

The slaves had moved the furniture and quickly turned the parlor into a small ballroom. The trio of musicians set up in the far corner.

Those not dancing or watching, mainly some of the men, had moved into the library. Some men and women also wandered into the dining room where the food had been displayed on the sideboard and additional small tables brought in. Slaves stood by to help, replenish the food, or quickly clean up when places were vacated.

Thankfully, the first dance didn't turn out to be a waltz, and Melanie breathed a sigh of relieve as she stepped around the other couple in their group. She caught sight of Toby dancing with his mother, but she dared not smile at him.

Lott danced three straight dances with her before she told him she needed some refreshments, and he led her to the dining room. After looking around the room and not seeing Toby, Lott left her, saying he wanted to find someone on a business matter.

Mrs. Askew came up to her. "This is a lovely party, my dear. I haven't been to an affair like this in years. But I was surprised to hear that you're planning to marry Mr. Jenkins. I hope you will be very happy." Her voice sounded tentative and held a lot of doubt.

"I do, too." Melanie lowered her voice. "I wasn't given much choice in the matter."

The older woman raised her eyebrows. "That doesn't sound like William."

"Just between you and me, I think William is facing some financial difficulties, and he thinks my marrying Mr. Jenkins will improve matters. He refuses to see any faults in the man and will hear nothing said against him."

"I'm so sorry." Mrs. Askew patted her hand. "I'll be praying for you, but is there anything else I can do?"

"Not that I can think of." Melanie wished she could do something.

"Well, if there ever is, you get me word. And I know I speak for my husband and son, as well."

Melanie finished her punch and wandered back into the parlor. A waltz started, but Lott didn't come to claim her as she expected.

Toby approached her instead. "Dance with me?"

She shook her head. "I dare not, Toby. It would be much too risky."

He put his hand on her back and guided her to the far end of the room, away from the library. "Lott's heavily ensconced in a business discussion. I just came from the library, and I don't think he will cause a scene in front of all these people. Come on, Mel. Dance with an old friend."

She didn't want to tell Toby Lott would take his anger out on her afterwards if he saw them together, so she nodded and slipped into his arms. He felt familiar and safe, and she questioned herself again. Maybe she should consider eloping with him, but that felt wrong to her. She wouldn't be that selfish or use him like that.

She enjoyed the dance more than any in a long time, since the one in the garden at Edenton in October to be exact. But she felt relieved when it ended without Lott appearing.

"Thank you," both she and Toby said at the same time.

She smiled. "Please let me go, and don't try to follow."

She knew he wasn't pleased, but he nodded. Surprisingly, she had a hard time walking away from him. She wondered if she would ever see him like this again and doubted it. Not if Lott had his way. That brought tears to her eyes, but she kept walking and didn't look back. She knew Toby would be standing where she'd left him, watching her the whole time.

Lott didn't reappear until a few minutes before midnight when the musicians struck up a waltz for the last dance. His firm hold and precise steps felt so different than Toby's. When the last note played, the musicians shouted "Happy New Year, everyone!" and Lott's lips lowered on hers. He didn't kiss her as roughly as he had before, but his tongue still probed her mouth, and he took his time.

She wondered if Lott wanted to make a show of kissing her for Toby to see. Sure enough, when she raised her head, Toby stood against the wall where he could see them plainly. The abject look of hurt on his face made her want to sob.

Toby didn't come over to say good-bye before they left. In fact, he disappeared quickly after the kiss at midnight.

Mrs. Askew came up instead. "Toby went to bring the carriage around. Thank you for a lovely evening." She turned to Constance with a smile. "You outdid yourself, dear. You have a real talent for entertaining."

Lott led Melanie from the entrance, leaving William and Constance to see the guests off. "You know, tradition says that the first person you kiss after midnight of the New Year will be the one you spend the most time with during that year." He smirked. "I'll be that man for you this year and every year to come."

She tried to return his smile, but it likely turned out to be weak at best.

When she said nothing, he continued. "I can't wait to see what you and Constance do for our engagement party. I want it much bigger and better than this."

"We'll do our best." She knew he expected some comment from her.

"I have some business to take care of from the contacts I made here tonight, but I'll see you soon." He kissed her cheek. "Stay away from that Askew boy, now."

Lott had chosen February the fourteenth as the date for their engagement ball. Constance had spared no expense, and the affair would undoubtedly be the talk of Winton and surrounding areas for years to come. Melanie didn't think any engagement anywhere could have been any more lavish.

None of this appealed to her. It seemed so showy and impersonal, but then impersonal might be good in this case. Just the thoughts of the aftermath of marrying Lott made her want to throw away all her resolve to not be selfish and to hold out for true love. Instead, she wanted to latch onto Toby and tell him to never let her go. Surely, true love wasn't just a fairy tale, however, but would she find it? Things certainly looked bleaker every day.

Gemona didn't help matters. She continued to push her case for eloping with Toby, and Melanie might have done that if she hadn't met Lucas at the masquerade ball. Although she knew there would be little hope of ever seeing the interesting man again, meeting him had shown her that there could be someone out there for her. Her heart didn't want to settle for anything less. She just hoped she didn't end up married to Lott and living under a mountain of regrets.

At Constance's insistence, Melanie spent half the day on the Saturday of the ball getting ready to go to Lott's. After a thorough bath, her new gold-colored dress turned her into a princess, and Gemona spent an exorbitant amount of time fashioning her hair.

Lott's eyes lit up the moment he saw her. "You look exquisite, darling. You'll have every woman here jealous, and I'll be the envy of every man."

"You look quite dashing yourself." And he did cut a nice figure in his impeccably tailored suit and every strand of his pale blond hair in place. But Melanie had become skilled in saying the correct thing by habit.

The night proceeded in a whirlwind where nothing seemed real. They greeted, ate, danced, talked, and laughed. The atmosphere had taken on a lightness that made it seem surreal, but Melanie decided just to enjoy the party without worry. She'd let tomorrow be soon enough for anxieties to burden her again.

She wished she could truly give everything to God and be completely free from burdens. But try as she might, she only partially succeeded. Did she lack trust in her Maker? If so, she'd need Him to help her with that, too.

This time Lott didn't leave her to discuss business, and to those who didn't know better, he must appear absolutely devoted to Melanie, but Melanie knew better.

He did what appealed to him at the time, whether he became attentive and concerned or angry and raging.

About half way through the evening, Lott stopped everything, got everyone's attention, and had William and Constance join them at the front. "I am the happiest man alive tonight." Lott smiled as his eyes swept over those in the room. "I get to announce that this beautiful creature..." He paused and reached over to pull Melanie to his side. "Has agreed to be my wife."

Applause broke out and a happy buzz spread about the room. Melanie plastered a smile on her face, and hoped it looked better than she felt. She had no idea that the official announcement would nauseate her so. After all, she'd known about this for months.

After dancing with Lott until her feet ached and speaking to the guests as they left, Lott walked Melanie to the door. Constance and William had discreetly gone to the carriage to wait for her.

"This has been a perfect night," Lott told her. "I hope you're as pleased as I am."

"Constance did most of the planning, but everything did look good."

"And you looked the best of anything." He lowered his head and she had no doubt the kiss he gave her would leave her lips bruised and swollen.

Chapter Twelve: News

"You've got to do something, Lucas." Glenna stomped into his office as if the newspaper in her hand had just announced the end of the world.

"Bad news, I take it." He often found his housekeeper's dramatics amusing.

"Indeed. Read it for yourself." She threw the copy of the *State Gazette of North Carolina* published in Edenton on his desk.

"The society page? You're showing me the society page?" She'd better not have some other affair she planned for him to attend.

Her finger came swiftly to rest on an engagement announcement: "Mr. William Carter of Winton announces the forthcoming wedding of his sister, Miss Melanie Carter, to Mr. Lott Jenkins also of Winton. The nuptials are scheduled for Sunday, June fifth, seventeen hundred and ninety-six at five o'clock in the afternoon."

The words became blurry, and he almost felt as if he were on the ship again, for the room seemed to be rocking. However, he dared not look at Glenna for fear that she would read his turbulent thoughts.

"You have to do something," she repeated.

"What can I do?" He tried to make his voice sound calm and unaffected, but he didn't think he succeeded.

"How can you be so calm?" Maybe he had succeeded. "We can't let this young woman be fed to the wolf."

Suddenly he pictured a young woman with creamy complexion and red hair instead of a red cape being accosted by a pale, snarling wolf, about ready to devour her. He shook his head. "This is not some fairy tale where I can rush in and save the maiden."

Glenna put her hands on her hips. "And why not?"

"Look at me." He turned his right side toward her, something he usually avoided, even with her. "I'm no Prince Charming – the beast maybe."

He knew he'd used the wrong analogy the moment he saw the gleam of triumph in Glenna's eyes. "And what did the beast do but turn into a prince the moment Beauty kissed his lips."

"Melanie will never kiss my lips after she sees what a hideous monster I've become." He hadn't lost this argument yet. The image of Melanie kissing him nearly undid him, however.

"You've become a monster all right. But it's not because of the scars on your skin but the ones on your heart and soul. You're becoming more selfish all the time, and it doesn't suit you. I want back the young man who thought of others and didn't think twice about the risk to himself if they needed help. I want the young man who didn't hesitate to speak out against injustice and let God direct his path." She waved her finger at him. "You need to think long and hard about this, Lucas Hall, because if that man maims or kills Melanie, it will be on your head."

"You don't need to be so melodramatic, Glenna." But Lucas didn't think she'd heard him. She'd already left the room, slamming the door behind her.

Lucas swiped the newspaper away. Even if he tried to help Melanie, his efforts would be futile. She'd told him how her brother refused to listen to reason, and a stranger's interference would only make matters worse for her. Hadn't he been through all this in his mind over and over again since the Edenton ball?

God, if there's something I can do to help Melanie Carter, please show me. I have no idea why I feel so drawn to her, but I would do anything to extract her from the clutches of Lott Jenkins, even bear exposing my scars to the world. Glenna is wrong. I'm not that selfish. I just honestly don't know what to do, how to help. If there's a way, Lord, please show me. Amen.

After pacing the small area in his office and getting no epiphany, he rang for Glenna and ordered a bottle of wine and a glass. He seldom drank, but he needed something to calm his erratic heart.

She didn't say a word but returned with a carafe of grape juice and a glass. She'd better watch it for he was in no mood for her obstinate defiance. "I said wine. Did you misunderstand?"

"You need your wits about you to figure this out." With that, she left.

He shook his head but still smiled at her antics. She kept him on the straight and narrow, refusing to let him get too far afield, and those were the qualities of a true friend or a real mother. Glenna had always been more of a mother to him than the woman who gave him birth. He'd only seen the woman he called "Mother" briefly when she felt it her duty and asked that he be presented before her.

His eyes landed on the crumpled newspaper on the floor. He picked it up ironed out the creases with his hands the best he could, and put it on the corner of his desk, getting black, ink-stained hands for his efforts.

Feeling completely helpless in the situation, he bowed his head again. *Lord, I'm at a loss here. I'm going to wait on Thee to show me what to do if I should act. I'm willing, but I need Thy direction. Show me Thy will, I pray. Amen.*

Lucas could have used a gallop on Jester, but the February weather hadn't cooperated lately, and sitting by the river fishing was out of the question.

He spent more time in the library than his office, because the newspaper still resting on the corner of his desk served as a constant reminder that time hadn't slowed, and the days were falling away.

Yet, his thoughts stayed on Melanie regardless of where he took himself. His mind tried to be logical and tell him he'd invested too much interest in a woman he'd only met once. So what if they'd had a good conversation and magical dance? Given the circumstances, that didn't mean a thing. Melanie had likely not given him a second thought, and, if they met again, her interest would surely have waned. Why, he didn't even know if she'd been attracted to him on their first meeting.

His heart didn't agree. Deep down he knew they had something so special developing that one meeting was all it took to know. It might not be logical, but on some level he'd never be able to explain, he knew. But he didn't know what to do about it.

A rare snowstorm blew in the first week in March, and left a pristine, white facade on everything. Underneath the clean-looking blanket, however, Lucas knew the same dead leaves, the same dirt, and the same imperfect world remained.

April brought too much rain, and he wondered if the farmers managed to get their seeds in the ground. He wondered more about Melanie and how she fared. Had she managed to keep the bright, happy glow he'd seen on her face when they danced, or had her situation weighed her down in depression? He prayed for her multiple times a day, but if God expected him to act, He hadn't told Lucas.

May brought warm days with the promise of the heat of summer, and the skies turned bright. Lucas rode all he wanted and went fishing, too. However, neither activity brought the respite he'd expected.

Glenna gradually warmed to him again, but at times he found her watching him as if she expected him to do something. He'd be glad to oblige if he had any idea what to do.

Perhaps he should don his suit of armor, ride in on his charger, and whisk her away to marry him. He would even do that if he thought it would help. But what if he rescued her only to find out she didn't care for him at all, especially when she learned of his scars. Then, her reputation would be ruined if he didn't marry her, and she would still be saddled with a husband she couldn't stand.

Lord, I need Thy help here. I have no idea what would be best. I feel like I'm stumbling around in the dark. Be my light, I pray. Illuminate my path; show me the way. I'm depending on Thee, and I have a feeling Melanie is, too. Don't let me fail her, Lord. Whatever I need to do, show me.

The situation and his confusion had certainly strengthened his prayer life. And he actually felt God's presence, so he had to believe God wouldn't fail Melanie.

"Time's slipping away." Glenna stated the obvious one evening at supper.

"I know."

"What are you going to do?"

"That I don't know." He looked at the woman. "What would you have me do? I keep thinking God will show me if he wants me to act, but I'm as dry of ideas as ever. What do you think would be best?"

"I've been thinking on it these months, and I think it would be best if you went to talk to Melanie's brother. I'm sure you have more money than Mr. Jenkins, and you could offer Mr. Carter a goodly sum to call off the wedding and allow you to court Melanie. That would give you two the time to get to know each other better and prevent her from having to marry against her wishes."

He paused to consider her suggestion. "That's not a bad idea, although I'll likely have my lawyer pay William a visit instead of going myself."

"If you went yourself, you'd likely get to see Melanie." The woman knew too much about negotiating. He should put her sharp mind to work in his businesses. "Besides, you'll have to allow Melanie to know about your accident at some point."

" Not necessarily. I can help her without expecting anything to develop between us. And even if it did, I wouldn't want to reveal the disgusting disfiguration in the beginning."

"It will be just as easy then as it will later on and may be even easier. But, if you insist, I could bandage your face as if you'd been recently injured."

"You're just full of ideas, aren't you?"

He couldn't decide if her eyes twinkled or shot daggers. Maybe some of both. "And I'll not be saying what you're full of."

It shocked him so much to hear something like that come from her mouth that he found himself speechless. He looked down at his plate and tried to finish his food, but it held no interest to him.

Finally, he pushed himself up. "I'll think on it."

"You do that. And remember that not everyone thinks your scars are repulsive. I don't"

"Why not, Glenna?" He had never understood it.

"I see the man beneath. Oh, I hurt that you had to go thought it all and how it's affected you, but you are so much more than a few scars. You are a wonderful man with so much to offer."

"But even you have to admit that most people are disgusted. They often stare at me in horror, like watching a chicken with its head cut off spurting blood. It's sickening but so ghastly they can't take their eyes off it. Or else, they turn away immediately from the sight too repugnant to look upon."

"You exaggerate, Lucas, but, yes, there are some people like that. However, there are others like me; but you'll never know them, because you give no one a chance. You will never know how Melanie will react if you refuse to take the chance with her."

How could he explain that if Melanie rejected him, it would be the end of any hopes, of all his dreams? He could handle never having her in his life better than he could deal with an outright rejection. Margaret Ann and his brother had killed so much of him, and each time someone turned from him, another piece died. If Melanie turned from him, too, he might be totally destroyed.

"I don't know." He didn't look at Glenna when he spoke. He didn't want to see the disappointment in her eyes. "These questions are too complicated for me to answer right now. I'm going up to my room."

He felt as if he were running from Glenna's probing when he hurried up the stairs and into his room. He sank into a cushioned chair and put his head in his hands.

Lord, I'm so afraid – afraid of rejection; afraid of losing Melanie, even though she's never been mine in any way; and afraid of stepping out and making myself vulnerable, the subject of ridicule, and a target for more hurt. Yet, I know fear is not pleasing to Thee, since the Bible states over and over again to fear not. Help me get beyond this hurt to be pleasing to Thee. I know I need to surrender all to Thee, but I need Thy help in even this. God, Thou promised that I could do all things through Thee, the One who strengthens me. Make it so, I pray. Amen.

He lifted his head to realize that, in this state, he wouldn't be the man Melanie needed. Determined to put her welfare above his own misgivings and insecurities, he decided he needed to go to Winton and confront William himself, the way Glenna had advised. He would offer the man any amount of money to free Melanie of Lott Jenkins, and then it would be up to her if she wanted to see him again or not.

He went over to his writing desk and took out a sheet of paper. He would have his investigator find out exactly where the Carters lived so he wouldn't have to go asking about and could ride straight to their house. Then he would go as soon as possible. June the twelfth was fast approaching.

Feeling drained, he got ready for bed and lay without covers. A gentle breeze floated in the window, cooling the room with the night's freshness. Crickets chirped as if they hadn't a care in the world. With one decision made, he drifted off to sleep.

Lucas rode faster than he ever had before in the breaking morning light. From the forest beside the open field, a horse and rider joined him. He looked at Melanie and smiled. He had prayed she would come, but he hadn't been sure. He slowed his horse to greet her.

"How is your face this morning?" Her eyes showed her concern.

He touched his cheek and felt the bandage Glenna had placed over the right side of his face before he left the house. He wore gloves to hide his hands. "It's healed a lot, but I'm afraid it will always be scarred."

She didn't appear worried. "I don't know how to thank you for what you've done for me. I've been praying for a miracle, but I never dreamed that would be you. I should have known, however. I've always seen you as my knight in shining armor."

He laughed, loving her teasing. "I'm just happy William accepted my offer. Do you expect Jenkins will cause trouble?"

Her happy expression fell into a frown, and he wanted to take the question back. He shouldn't have mentioned Jenkins at all this morning.

"I'm afraid he may. He's not a man to accept defeat." She started her horse moving at a pace slow enough they could still talk, and he followed at her side.

"Then I'll make sure you have bodyguards to protect you."

"Why, Lucas? Why are you doing this?"

"You've begun to mean something special to me." He gave her a sideways glance. "And I hope someday you will feel the same about me. But as for now, I have no expectations."

"A special friend?" She asked it as a question, and he knew what she meant.

"That's a good start." He hoped those words would convey he wanted more without actually saying it and scaring her away. Before he asked if she would allow him to court her, he needed to reveal his scars. He hoped to do that this morning if he could get up the nerve.

"I'll race you to the river." She kicked her horse as she said it, and he took off a second after her.

They rode neck and neck, as if the cool morning breeze carried them along. He had dreamed of this for so long, riding across a meadow with Melanie by his side.

In no time, she drew up her horse, laughing in complete joy. His heart sang with her laughter.

He slipped from his saddle and went to hand her off her horse. He saw a slave in the distance watching, but the man made no attempt to come close. Of course, she would bring a chaperone.

His heart went wild when he placed his hands on her tiny waist to help her down. His whole body reacted when she ended up standing so close to him they almost touched.

He took a step back, knowing he needed to act the gentleman, but his arms ached to wrap around her and his lips begged him to kiss her. That would come later. He hoped.

They moved to a log near the forest and sat down. He picked up her hand, hoping her touch would give him the courage to pull off the bandages.

"I've thought about you often since the masquerade ball." She looked at their clasped hands as if embarrassed by the admission.

"Oh, yes?"

She continued as he hoped she would. "Remembering the magical time has given me moments of happiness, even when the situation looked gloomy."

"I'm glad. I've often recalled that night as well." He gave her hand a gentle squeeze. "When I saw the engagement announcement in the newspaper, I became worried about you."

"I'm so glad you came."

Her eyes held an emotion he dared not call "love," but it looked close. The time had come.

He began slowly removing the bandage. "I need to show you my scarred face. Several years ago, I was in the military in England, and a cannon blew up beside me during a training exercise. It shouldn't have had that much powder in it. The doctors thought I might die, but I pulled through, although I'll never look the same."

He stopped there with the explanation. He could tell her about Margaret Ann and his brother later if she could handle his disfigurement. If not, he wouldn't need to tell her anything.

She gasped in disbelief, and her hands flew to her mouth to prevent a cry of horror. She closed her eyes, and he knew. He closed his as well.

When he felt movement beside him, he looked to see her hurrying toward her horse. She picked up the reins and ran for the slave, who now also ran toward her. Lucas watched the man lift her into the saddle. She didn't look back once as she rode away.

He let her go. He planned to sit there until his legs would hold him and then he'd need to go home. His worst nightmare had just happened, but he could do nothing to get out of it.

Lucas awoke and sat up in bed, hoping to distance himself from what must have been a dream. But it had seemed so real. Had it been a dream or a forewarning of what would come?

He lit the candle beside his bed to dispel some of the darkness. The clock showed four o'clock, so he might as well stay up. He certainly didn't want to go back to sleep and chance another horrible dream.

He picked up his Bible and held it closer to the light. He could use some words of wisdom now, something to erase the despair the nightmare had caused.

Chapter Thirteen: At the Plantation

With her wedding approaching at an alarming pace, Melanie tried not to let herself get into a panic or become too depressed. The fact that she'd seen less and less of Lott as the date drew nearer helped. He said he had business that required his attention, but Melanie wondered if he felt secure that she would marry him now that the official announcement had been made and didn't feel the need to woo her any longer. He'd even had the announcement placed in the Edenton newspaper.

Whatever the reason, however, it made her life more bearable. Perhaps it would be the same if they married, and he'd be gone much of the time on business. She couldn't bring herself to think "when" they married, for she still hoped and prayed for a miracle.

On gloomy days when the burden of it all felt oppressive, she took out Toby's letters, reread them, and prayed.

Gemona handed her the first one at the end of February. She'd ripped into it, eager to see what he'd say. She had feared she'd never hear from him again after he didn't say good-bye at the New Year's ball, but at least he had written.

Dear Mellie,

Please forgive my churlish behavior at your New Year's party. I can't begin to explain the emotions I felt when I saw Jenkins kiss you like that, but that is no excuse for treating you so poorly. I know you need my support and understanding and not my selfish pouts.

I feel so helpless. Apart from the offers I've already made, I can't think of anything, except maybe to see that Jenkins meets with an accident, but my Christian conscience will not allow me such actions.

I wish you would accept my offer, but if we are to remain friends, I realize that I must respect your wishes. However, if you can come up with anything I might do to help, any plan that would set you free, please count me in. Know that I would do anything to insure your happiness.

Please answer this brief letter as soon as you can. I need to know if I have your forgiveness.

Your friend forever,
Toby

Melanie wiped her tears away. Toby hadn't been angry with her as she assumed, and he wanted to ask her forgiveness.

"He's upset you?" Melanie had forgotten about Gemona.

She shook her head. "No, but he's just so sweet."

"That's what I've been telling you. Now are you ready to run off with the fellow and give him the joy he deserves?"

Melanie looked back down at the letter. Oh how tempting that sounded, but she shook her head. "That happiness would only be temporary. He'd feel worse when he realizes I'll never see him as more than a friend."

Gemona just left the room, mumbling and shaking her head.

Melanie got out her paper, pen, and ink. She would answer Toby right away. She didn't know how Gemona went about getting the letters back and forth, and she didn't want to know. The slaves had all kinds of networks, and it would be better if few people knew about them.

Dear Toby,

Of course I forgive you, although there is little to forgive. I feared that you were upset with me, and that grieved me. I don't want to lose our friendship, but I don't know how much longer we can have any contact.

However, that makes the time we have all the more precious.

I am keeping your letters to read over and over again. I may need them to remind me that I have one true friend, besides Gemona. Therefore, don't write anything that could be misconstrued should they fall into the wrong hands. I feel I can be a bit freer in what I say, however.

I'd like you to know how much our dance at the New Year's party meant to me. Since Lott didn't discover us, I'm glad you pushed me into it. I remember when we used to dance as children, teaching each other what we knew. You made me feel safe and secure for the time that we danced on New Year's Eve, and I needed that.

I forget to tell you how much our friendship means to me. It's rare to have childhood friends who stay so close as adults, especially when one is male and the other female. No matter what happens to me, I want you to find your happiness. Even if there comes a time when I can no longer have any contact with you, please know that I'm thinking of you, praying for you, and willing you to be happy.

Don't be sad for me. God has me in His care no matter what happens, no matter how bleak things appear. And, no, I'm not giving up. I'm still expecting a miracle.

Your forever friend,

Melanie

Since that first letter, they had come at regular intervals with at least one a week, Most of them just talked about what he'd been doing, matters of the farm, and where he'd gone – things he would have told her if they could meet. But that's what she needed. She needed to be grounded in his ordinary life in order to keep her mind off where hers seemed to be headed.

She wrote him back the same day, making comments about what he'd told her, teasing him about his mistakes, and telling him about the better parts of her days.

"William, are you going out to the plantation soon?" Melanie looked at her brother over the breakfast table. He normally went about three or four times a week now that planting had begun.

"I plan to go early tomorrow morning and spend the day. Why?"

"Would you take me with you? I'd like to spend a day in the country."

Constance wrinkled her nose. "Whatever for? There's not even a decent house there in which to rest or have dinner."

"I want to go riding and maybe fishing. I have a lot of memories there from my childhood and of my parents. I guess I'm feeling nostalgic, but I'd like a long visit before the wedding. It will be good just to see the place again."

"I can understand." William looked at his wife. "I'd miss the plantation, too, if I hadn't been back for any length of time. We lived there for longer than we've lived here, and there's a part of us that will always see it as home." He turned back to Melanie. "Of course you can come. Just be up and ready by six o'clock."

"And be sure you don't meet anyone while fishing." Now Constance had begun to sound like Lott.

Gemona didn't complain at all about getting up so early, which surprised Melanie. Melanie even enjoyed eating a quick breakfast with William. She knew William had found someone he could be happy with in Constance, but her sister-in-law often added tension to the table. And Constance had quickly become Lott's strongest ally and supporter.

The day looked foggy and overcast as they started off, but Melanie knew it would turn sunny from the lightening in the eastern sky. Gemona and Jericho accompanied them. Both slaves would stay with Melanie to see to her protection and needs.

"You won't become bored before the day is over?" William had been silent for most of the trip, but Melanie didn't mind. Neither of them had to talk to be comfortable.

Melanie chuckled. "No. I brought a book and some needlework just in case, but I doubt I even pull them out. I'm looking forward to the outside activities today."

He smiled. "Sometimes I forget what a tomboy you used to be, still are to some degree, I guess, behind that very feminine exterior. I can see why Lott chose you, Mel. You've turned into a very beautiful young woman."

"Thank you." Melanie just wished she could forget about Lott and the impending marriage for today, but William didn't give her many compliments, which made the ones he did give all the more special.

In many ways, the day turned out to be everything Melanie wanted. She went riding first, racing through the fields at full-speed. She liked feeling the wind on her face and her hair blowing out behind her. Jericho tried to keep up, but Gemona didn't even try.

It would have been better if she could have ridden astride, like she had as a child with Toby, but she'd had to make concessions to adulthood and proper behavior. And she would take riding any way she could get it. She liked the taste of freedom it gave her, and a sense of freedom and independence came so seldom these days. She wondered if Lott would let her ride like this and then chided herself for thinking of the man.

The three of them went fishing, and Melanie enjoyed the time, but it seemed strange not to have Toby join them. She looked at Gemona. "I'm surprised you didn't tell Toby we'd be here today."

The slave jutted out her chin in that stubborn way Melanie had come to expect. "I did, but he said he would honor your wishes not to see him secretly. He said he enjoyed your letters and didn't want to do anything to jeopardize them."

Melanie smiled at her maid's failed manipulations, but a part of her would love to see Toby again, especially to fish with him.

They went back to the plantation to meet William for dinner. Cook had packed them a picnic and Melanie planned to eat beneath one of the big oak trees which still stood in front of the house's charred remains.

She enjoyed the time with her brother and listening to him talk about the plantation and the crops, but she regretted that Gemona and Jericho couldn't eat with them. They'd have to wait until she and William had finished before they ate.

By the time William left to go back to work, the two slaves had also eaten. Gemona packed everything away, while Melanie stayed underneath the old oak tree. She looked at the spot where her childhood home had stood. The fire, time, and the weather had taken their toll, only leaving the crumbling foundation and portions of the chimneys.

Memories from the past swept through her mind like actors on a revolving stage. Although Mother had been determined to make a lady out of her wayward daughter, Papa had no doubt she would be a lady of quality in the end. In the meantime, he'd let her roam the property, discover the truths all around her, and learn as much as she desired.

It had been he who had kept William's tutor on just to later teach her. He had agreed to let Toby join her in the schoolroom, and they'd soon become inseparable.

Her life would have been so much different now if her father had lived. He would have never allowed her to marry a man like Lott. Papa would have seen right through him.

She sighed, and wiped the moisture from her eyes. Wishing for what might have been brought no respite to her troubles.

The day had become hot and humid, making it uncomfortable to move about. Again, she wished she could be a girl again, wearing only a cool shift over a minimum of undergarments. The stays and all the layers she wore now made the day even more unpleasant.

She heard a commotion coming from behind the barn and went to investigate with Jericho and Gemona following a few steps behind. The unmistakable crack of a whip gave her some indication of what might be happening, but she still grimaced when she came upon the scene.

Willis Brickle, the overseer, stood over a slave stripped to the waist and tied to a post. By the looks of the man's back, he'd already received three lashes.

"What's going on here?" Melanie made sure her voice rang with authority.

Brickle's hand halted in midair with his whip falling from its intended path to the man's back, glistening in sweat and striped with three long gashes.

"Isn't it obvious?" Every muscle in his body seem to tense from anger, but she could tell he fought not to lose control.

She had no doubt he would love to send that whip flying her way. "Why are you flogging this man?"

"He refused to work, but you have no right to question me." He had dropped his hand to his side, but he clenched the whip even tighter.

"You know who I am?"

"I do." He spat as if to say that's what he thought of her. "You're William Carter's younger sister, but he's given me full control over how I handle the slaves."

Melanie moved around so she could see the restrained slave's face. "Did you refuse to work?"

The man wouldn't look at her and didn't answer.

"You understand that I'm your mistress." She looked at Brickle to make sure he didn't disagree. "You won't be punished for answering me. Will he, Mr. Brickle?"

"No, Miss." No doubt the man regretted the words, but he forced them out anyway.

She turned back to the slave. "What's your name?"

"Hardy, Miss…"

"Melanie." Gemona supplied from behind her. "You can call her Miss Melanie."

"All right, Hardy. Did you refuse to work?"

"No, Miss Melanie. I's just goin' for de water bucket fo' a drank. It be mighty hot out today. Mister Brickle holler at me to git back ta work, and I's start to tell him I needs some water in a powerful way, but he have me brought here and tied."

She looked at Brickle. "Is this true?"

"I told him to get back to work, and he didn't. If I don't make the slaves obey me immediately, things will get out of hand, and the work will never get done."

"How many lashes do you plan to give him?"

"Forty is the usual number for disobedience."

Melanie felt sure she had grown pale, despite the heat. "I think three will suffice fine for today, since Hardy didn't intend to disobey you." She quickly turned to the slaves before Brickle could protest.

"Untie him. Is Maude still here?" A number of slaves nodded. "Hardy, you go to Maude's cabin and get her to put some of her healing ointment on those wounds, drink plenty of water, and rest for the rest of the afternoon."

"Yes'm." His eyes told her how much he thanked her, although he appeared afraid to say it aloud.

"What about her, Miss Melanie?" Gemona pointed to a young woman restrained between two burly men.

Melanie had failed to notice her before. "Were you going to flog her, too?"

"She refused to go to my place to clean up and fix me supper." Brickle's tone filled with indignation and bordered on belligerence.

"Is your wife unable to cook your supper?"

"I took her and the kids to her folks Sunday to stay for a couple of weeks. They do that every summer."

Melanie looked at the attractive slave who looked to be younger than Melanie. Her eyes were wide with fear, and she quivered beneath the men's hold.

"Why did you refuse to do what Mr. Brickle asked?"

"I don't mind cookin' and cleanin', but he 'spect me to spend the night." Her voice squeaked with fear. She looked down at the ground. "He woulda had me stripped to the waist here, too, in order to whips me"

"This is unacceptable." Melanie made her voice as hard as possible. "I will take this matter up with William, and I'd better not hear of you mistreating another slave. You'd better not try to retaliate with Hardy or this young woman either. Discipline is one thing, but unwarranted abuse is another."

Brickle wouldn't look at her. She hoped he felt too embarrassed, but she doubted it. "I'll take this up with William, too. We'll see what he has to say."

Melanie watched the slaves move back to the field. She wondered who Brickle left in charge while he came to the whipping post, because she knew most of the slaves must have stayed there.

If Melanie had felt lethargic before, a combination of the heat and the upheaval Brickle had created drained her. She went back to the shade of the oak tree. Maybe she would read or do some needlework until William got ready to go back.

"You shouldn't have interfered, Mel." Apparently Brickle had gone straight to William with his version of what had happened.

"I couldn't watch two slaves be beaten to the bone for such paltry reasons."

"They disobeyed the overseer, and he has to keep control. He and his family could be in danger if he doesn't."

"You probably didn't get the full version of what happened." Melanie proceeded to tell him exactly what she had learned.

He first paled and then grew red in the face when Melanie told him Brickle had expected the pretty young slave to spend the night with him. "This is exactly why I don't want you involved. A lady shouldn't even know of such things."

She couldn't believe William. She tells him about injustice and immorality, and all he can think about is protecting her from such knowledge. "That doesn't change the fact that Brickle mishandled the situation at best and is possibly depraved and evil."

"Just let it go, Mel. I'll have a word with him, but it happens." He put up his hand to stop her protest. "I don't like it either, but without living on the plantation, there's little I can do. I can't be there to see to things, and I need Brickle."

"Find another overseer." Melanie wouldn't give up so easily. "I think I heard Mrs. Askew say that Randall would love to find another job. The one he has doesn't pay much, and it's not steady. If you remember, as the oldest son, he's always been the most responsible one of the boys. And I'm sure his wife and two little ones would enjoy living on the plantation."

William looked at her strangely. "I'll give it some thought. In fact, I might call Randall in for an interview. His farming background would be helpful, and all the Askew boys are strong Christians. I just don't know if Randall would be tough enough to keep the slaves in line."

"Toby would tell you he would. Randall's had plenty of experience helping keep his younger brothers in line. I can attest to the fact that he can be hard and stern when needed."

William nodded and she thought he planned to end the conversation, but Melanie felt better. She would feel better still if Randall Askew took the overseer's position.

"I'm beginning to regret bringing you out to the plantation today." She'd been wrong, because William hadn't finished the conversation. "I had no idea you would be so disruptive or get involved with an issue you had no business even knowing about."

"I'm beginning to regret going, too. I'm seeing a side of my brother that appalls me." She bit her tongue too late. She shouldn't have said that. It would only serve to enrage William and do nothing to help her plight. In fact, if she kept talking like that, he'd likely be eager to hand her over to Lott.

"This has been some day, hasn't it?" Gemona
stood behind Melanie brushing her hair out before
bedtime.

"Yes, it has. I really enjoyed this morning. I hate
that I had to confront Brickle this afternoon, but I'm
praying some good will come from it."

"At least you tried your best. Jericho and I were
proud of you."

"Thanks. That means a lot." It surprised Melanie
how much. When was the last time someone said they
were proud of her? Not since her parents had died.

Chapter Fourteen: Intruder

Toby Askew stood in the church yard with a group of men while he watched for Melanie. He knew better than try to speak to her, but he just wanted a quick glance to see that she looked all right. He had always been able to know how happy or troubled she was.

She came out with William, and her eyes found his for just a moment, but the brief smile she sent his way told him all he needed to know. Jenkins didn't accompany her, which had become the usual state of affairs. And Constance stayed confined to the house now due to the baby that should arrive soon.

All the men, except Cornelius Phelps, gradually left to collect their families and go home. Toby started to do the same when Phelps stopped him.

"You wouldn't need an indentured servant, would you? Ann and I have decided to go back to England where we still have family, and I'll make you a good price. James still has five years left on his indenture, and he's experienced at farming."

The price he named turned out to be less than half
what indentured servants usually went for, and Toby had
that much saved. He had been wondering how he could
have some free time to take care of a personal matter,
and this appeared to be the answer.

"Could I meet the man first?"

"Sure, but I'll do you one better. I'll bring him by
your place tomorrow, and let you put him to work. I'll
come back Wednesday, and you can either pay me or I'll
take him back."

"That sounds like a deal." They shook on it.

James Wynns turned out to be twenty-eight and
looked strong, although not large. After they'd talked a
few minutes, Phelps left the servant and rode away,
leading the horse Phelps had come on.

Toby took James to the barn. "I'm going to show
you around, but I want to talk to you a minute first. You
will be responsible to my father when I'm away, and I
have some business to take care of. You have five years
left on your indenture, but if you work hard and we're
pleased, I'll release you after no more than three."

His eyes brightened, and Toby had his full
attention as he showed him around and introduced him
to the family. He had already discussed it with his
parents. His father didn't understand why he wanted to
do this, and Toby couldn't explain; but the elder Askew
said if the man did the work, he'd have no complaints.

James turned out to be the hardest worker Toby had ever seen. He did more work on Tuesday than any of the Askews ever had in one day, and none of them were sluggards.

Therefore, he gladly paid Phelps for the indenture on Wednesday and rode out headed southeast on Friday. He had no idea how long this would take, but Gemona had a good point. They couldn't sit by, do nothing, and see Melanie tied to a man who would make her miserable.

At least the warm weather would allow him to camp out some of the time. He'd brought enough supplies that his horse looked more like a pack animal than a mount, but he felt a surge of excitement as he said his good-byes and rode away. *Lord, grant me success, I pray.*

The man Lucas had hired to find Melanie's exact location had sent him the information days ago, and still he procrastinated. Before his accident, he had considered himself courageous and bold when circumstances warranted, but now fear and uncertainty wanted to control him.

Somehow, he knew his whole future would depend on the moment he confronted Melanie and her brother, and, after that nightmare, he feared the outcome. He tried to tell himself he'd be no worse off than now, but that wasn't true. Melanie's rejection would destroy so much of what remained of Lucas Hall that only a shell would be left.

He tried to tell himself how ridiculous it was to give so much power to a woman he had met but once. What did he really know about Melanie Carter? She could be spoiled and selfish like Margaret Ann for all he knew. But on some level he didn't understand, his heart knew.

He tried to tell himself to trust God more, but that didn't help either. He knew what he needed to do, what he wanted to do, but doing it didn't come as easily. He examined himself to determine if he'd put Melanie above God in his life, but decided he hadn't. No, he loved God more, for he didn't even know if he loved Melanie yet. But somehow, he felt God had sent Melanie into his life for a purpose. That should have given him great hope, but it didn't. God might just want to use her to teach him some important lessons.

Finally, Lucas felt he could put it off no longer, and he made plans to leave on the twenty-ninth of May, nearly a week away. He would spend all day Saturday traveling, and go to the Carters on Sunday afternoon. That would give him the best chance of speaking to William and Melanie.

He would have Glenna bandage his scars. He just hoped the outcome would be different than in the dream, but he couldn't dispel a sinking feeling.

"Miles Hill just said to tell you he found signs of someone trespassing on the estate."

"Really?" Miles Hill was his groundskeeper.

"Have Miles come in. I want to question him." Lucas reached for his hangman's mask. This wouldn't be the first time Miles had seen him in it.

"What did you see?" Lucas asked the forty-something man sitting in the chair across from his desk.

"Just some footprints, some broken twigs on bushes, and an area near the river where it looked like someone has stayed for at least a few hours."

"Where did the footprints lead?"

Miles shifted in his seat. "Mainly to the house and back."

Lucas sat back to digest the information he didn't want to hear. At least the drapery on the one window in his office stayed drawn. The only other place he went without a mask was in his suite, and that would be hard to see into on the second floor.

But then he did go about the house bare-faced after the servants left for the day and before they returned again. He let out a long breath. "Do you think the man is planning mischief, perhaps to rob the place?"

"It's hard to tell, but I don't think anyone who'd sneak around like this is up to any good."

Again, not information Lucas wanted to hear. "Well, be vigilant. Hire more men to guard the place if you need to." At least Miles had a caretaker's cottage and stayed on the property. He trusted the man to take care of things. The fact that Miles had figured out they'd an intruder proved that trust well-founded.

"Maybe I should postpone the trip to Winton until after this situation with an intruder eases." William looked over at Glenna as they finished their dessert at supper.

"And that's not apt to happen until after Melanie is married. Then there'd be no need to go." She was right, of course. "You go ahead with your plans. We'll be fine. Miles will make sure nothing happens, and your trip should only take three days at the most."

He nodded. "I'll need you to bandage my face Saturday morning before I leave."

"That, I'll do. I'll go with you, now, if you want."

He gave that a moment's thought but then shook his head. "No. It's better if I go alone." On one hand, he'd liked to have Glenna's support and sage advice, but on the other hand he'd need to be alone in his misery if Melanie turned from him in disgust the way she had in the dream.

Friday, Melanie walked in the garden. She just needed to get out of the house for a while. William had remained reticent since her thoughtless remark in the carriage. On top of that, Lott was due back from a business trip tomorrow, and he wouldn't be leaving again before the wedding.

"Let's go fishing," Gemona suggested. "Maybe it will bring you some peace and put a smile on your face for a change."

"All right." What could it hurt? Watching the river usually soothed her, and the shady spot she liked would be cooler. "Tell Jericho, and I'll go put on an old dress."

"That dress will be fine."

Melanie looked at Gemona in surprise. Her maid usually told her not to dirty her good clothes, and this was one of her newer dresses, apart from her trousseau. But, since she didn't feel like taking the time to change, she gladly didn't bother.

Jericho took them to the river, saw them settled, and then said he needed to pick up some things for the plantation at the blacksmith. He promised not to be long.

Gemona became unusually quiet, and Melanie sat watching the river more than her pole. She felt like one of those leaves in water. It became caught in the current and swept away without any say in the matter and too weak to fight against it. She hadn't given up hope that she'd still get her miracle, but it looked less likely with each passing day.

Gemona sat with her eyes closed, and her head began to nod. Melanie felt more relaxed than she had in weeks, so perhaps she'd let herself take a quick nap, as well.

Suddenly she heard movement and looked up to see a hooded man standing over her with a gun pointed. "You need to come with me."

His raspy voice sounded odd, like he wanted to disguise it, but Melanie didn't have time to ponder that now. She couldn't believe this. Gemona now appeared wide awake, her eyes like saucers.

Melanie swallowed. "This must be some mistake."

The man just shook his head and wiggled the gun to say they should move downstream.

Melanie looked at Gemona. "T-that gun makes me think we need to do what the man says." Gemona's voice quivered.

Melanie couldn't think of any other course of action, so she started walking on the narrow path cut by hundreds of feet over the years. Going in this direction would mean they'd be less likely to be seen, but that didn't mean she wouldn't yell and draw attention the minute she thought someone might hear.

"You make undue noise, and I'll have to kill you," the man croaked out, as if he had read her mind.

The man didn't push them to move too fast but let them take their time, especially through some thickets. Although he walked behind them, she looked at him whenever she had a chance. He wore a black, hooded mask, much like a hangman might have worn in the days of castles and knights. Something about him looked vaguely familiar, but she couldn't watch him long enough to figure it out.

They must have walked a mile or so before they came to two horses tied to trees. Each one had bulging saddlebags and rolled-up blankets behind the saddle.

The man lifted Melanie into the saddle, and she tried to see his eyes through the holes in his mask, but he kept them averted. She had no chance to ride away, because the horse remained tied. The man turned, lifted Gemona behind Melanie, gathered the reins, and mounted. Gemona clutched Melanie, as if she thought she might go tumbling to the ground at any moment.

Jericho would return for them soon, and when he found only their fishing poles, he'd rush to inform William. Men would be searching for them before the hour was out. She relaxed a little.

Now that the man rode in front, Melanie had a chance to watch him carefully. The way he sat a horse almost reminded her of …. No, it couldn't be. It absolutely couldn't be.

They skirted all the houses, and Melanie didn't see anyone to call to, but the man kept his gun close. They eventually came to a road. She looked around her for several minutes. Was this the road to Colerain? Considering the direction they were traveling, it had to be. At least there wouldn't be as many swamps in this direction.

They stopped just before dark, and the man tied them to young trees before he began making camp. After he'd heated some food over a campfire, he untied them. When he put his hand on her arm to guide her, she looked at him. "Toby Askew! What do you think you are doing?"

He froze and then shook his head. "I knew I wouldn't fool you." He yanked the mask from his head.

"Have you lost your wits? Why would you kidnap me?"

"It's the only way I could think of to save you from Jenkins."

"Knowing that my reputation will be ruined, is this your way of forcing me to marry you?" Her anger had grown to dangerous proportions.

He looked aghast. "No, Mellie, I wouldn't do that. Besides, I don't think your reputation will be ruined, since you have Gemona with you. I hope not."

Realizing he had intended to help her in some misguided fashion, her ire began to cool. "You are going to be in so much trouble. If William doesn't kill you, I have no doubt Lott will."

"It would be worth it if this frees you from Jenkins. I would do just about anything to keep you from marrying him."

She gave a little snort. "I think you just proved that."

"Are you mad at me?"

He reminded her so much of the boy he'd been years ago. "Yes." But she knew the tone of her voice belied the word.

"You threatened to shoot us." Her anger rekindled.

"You know I could have never done that. It was a threat, nothing more. Come, let's eat before the food is completely cold."

"I'm not sure I want to." She tried to pull back the smile that wanted to burst across her face. "You never could cook anything fit to eat, even over a campfire."

"I still cook better than you."

She couldn't argue with that. When she started eating, she found herself hungrier than she thought.

Toby grinned at her. "Do you want another serving? It must not have tasted too bad."

She chose not to answer. "What are your plans now? When do we go back?"

Toby shifted around. "I haven't made a lot of plans, but I don't think we should go back until the date for the wedding passes."

"But that's two weeks away. Surely you don't expect me to camp out with you for that long."

He shifted again and looked at his hands clasped together as if he hoped they'd give him some sort of answer. "I'll find us a place to stay tomorrow. Right now, we need to get some rest. I don't know about you, but I've had a tiring day."

"If I had a rock close, I'd hurl it at you for that last remark." She wanted to ask him what sort of place would he be looking for, but she let it drop for now.

He grinned. "I know you would."

"I am tired, so if you brought bedding, I think I will retire."

He got up. "Can I trust you not to run off, or do I need to tie you again."

"Where am I going to go in the middle of the night with only a sliver of a moon this far away from home? Give me a little credit for having some sense."

Gemona helped her get situated. "At least it's Toby, and we'll be safe with him," she whispered to Melanie.

Although her body ached with tiredness, Melanie couldn't get to sleep. The ground felt especially hard and lumpy beneath her blanket, the mosquitoes wouldn't leave her alone, and she couldn't quit thinking about Toby and what he'd done. She feared no good would come from this.

Gemona didn't have any trouble falling to sleep. With her blanket right beside Melanie's, she could hear the woman's gentle snore. Sometime in the late night or early morning, Melanie must have joined her.

Melanie awoke to the sounds and smells of Toby cooking a breakfast of cornmeal mush, not her favorite, but she wouldn't complain. She still couldn't get it into her head that Toby had kidnapped her. It didn't line up with the man she knew as a dear friend.

After everything had been cleared away, he looked at Melanie. "I need to go into Colerain to get more supplies since I couldn't bring that much on the horses. I'll also look for a place for us to stay."

Something about his demeanor looked shamed, and, as he continued, Melanie knew why. "I'm going to have to tie you up while I'm gone, and I'll have to take you a distance off the road."

"No, Toby." Melanie didn't want to be bound for hours. "What if I give you my word I won't try to escape?"

He thought and looked torn. "No," he finally said. "I have to be sure Lott can't find you before the wedding."

"You don't trust me?" Now she felt truly hurt.

"I'm not sure I wouldn't try to escape in your position, and we're a lot alike. I would tell myself that since I'd been taken against my will, the situation warranted unusual behavior."

Her spirit fell. "I guess we're not as much alike as you think."

Chapter Fifteen: Escape

They rode farther than Melanie expected and ended up deep within a wooded area. Toby tied both her and Gemona to a tree.

"I've tried to make the knots tight but leave the rope loose enough that it won't cut into you. I shouldn't be long."

"I don't know why I ever thought him one of my two best friends," Melanie grumbled to Gemona. "I guess I should be grateful that he didn't gag us and we can still talk to each other."

"He's doing this for your own good." Gemona would still hear no wrong against Toby.

"Well, he has misplaced values, logic, or whatever. I'm afraid this will only make things worse for all of us, and especially him."

"We don't have to tell who did this. He didn't intend for you to know, but you had to go and recognize him."

"I won't lie, and I can't believe you approve of what he did." Melanie stared at the dark woman, trying to determine what she could be thinking.

"You can probably get by without lying. Just say that the man had a hooded-mask over his head and didn't talk much."

Melanie just shook her head. To be honest, she didn't want to get Toby in deep trouble. One incident of bad judgment couldn't erase years of friendship. But she didn't know about lying, even lying by omission. She'd have to pray on it.

Melanie closed her eyes, and Gemona sat quietly for a while, probably realizing that Melanie needed to pray.

"You know Rahab lied to save the Israelite spies, and God blessed her for her actions." Gemona knew her Bible and used it often.

"I'm not sure he approves you using the Bible to support your opinions, though."

"Why not if it's true? I think it's wrong to lie when it's to your advantage – it gets you out of trouble for something you did or gives you something you want – but I think it's different when you do it to help others."

"Like Rahab did?" Melanie asked it as a question.

"Exactly."

"I'm still not sure I agree. I'll think about it."

"Now, what Peter did when he lied about knowing Jesus was wrong." Gemona didn't want to drop the topic. "He lied to protect his own hide, because he became scared."

"I understand what you're saying." Melanie had grown tired of this discussion. "I'll give it consideration." She leaned her head back against the tree and closed her eyes, hoping Gemona would get the message.

Melanie opened her eyes a little later to see Gemona squirming and twisting her arms. "How tight are your ropes? Mine seem to have loosened up some since Toby tied us."

Melanie tried to move her hands, and sure enough, the ropes felt looser than she expected. "I think I can wiggle my hands out." She made her hands as narrow as she could and managed to get one out. Then the other one came out easily.

Melanie rubbed her wrists where they had scraped against the rough hemp. Then, she went to untie Gemona.

"What are you going to do? Don't you think it would be safer to stay here until Toby gets back?" Gemona must have known Melanie had no intention of staying here, for it sounded like a half-hearted suggestion.

Toby had left one horse tied nearby, but Melanie didn't know how she would mount it with her skirts getting in the way. However, she had no intention of giving up. She would lead the horse in the direction she thought she could find the river. If she could get to the river, she could follow it to someone who could help her.

On the way, maybe she would come to a stump or something she could use as a mounting block, although there didn't seem to be any trees felled in this area. If she had to, she would pull up her skirts and get Gemona to give her a boost into the saddle. Then, maybe with her pulling, Gemona could mount using the stirrup.

Melanie had almost given up hope of finding anything to help her step up into the saddle, when they came to a tree uprooted from some storm, and partially resting on another tree. If she led the horse up beside it, it would be an angular path into the saddle.

Gemona held the horse steady, and Melanie had no trouble walking up the wide trunk and climbing onto the horse. She took the reins and kept the horse still while Gemona followed.

With a smile on her face they set off, and it didn't take long to clear the woods. She would have loved to gallop along the river with the pretty meadow to her right, but she didn't for Gemona's sake.

"Hold it right there," someone shouted. Melanie had just started to rein in her horse to see if the man could help them, when she caught the glimpse of a snake slithering across her path. The horse reared in fear, and Melanie lost her seat. The last thing she remembered was hitting the ground and not being able to breath.

Glenna came running into Lucas's office so out of breath she could hardly get her words out. "Miles found … a lady … and her maid … on the … property. The lady's injured. The maid says she's Melanie Carter."

Lucas jumped up. "Where are they?"

Miles carried the woman here, and the maid followed. I put them upstairs in a guest room. Melanie fell from her horse and is unconscious. I sent for Dr. Winston, who's visiting with his sister in town."

Lucas sank back into his chair. Melanie was here? In his home? He couldn't believe it.

"See that she receives the best of care. I'd appreciate it if you would look after her yourself as much as you can."

Glenna nodded her agreement. "Aren't you going up to see her?"

"Not right away." He needed to give this unexpected turn of events more thought. "I'm depending on you."

A puzzled looked worried Glenna's face, but she nodded again, and hurried back upstairs. Lucas closed his eyes and prayed.

Glenna grabbed Mary, one of the maids on her way up the stairs. It would be good to have her there in case fetching needed to be done. She paused before the bedroom door and took a deep breath to calm herself. It wouldn't do to be scaring her guests now.

She opened the door to find Gemona bending over Melanie applying a blood-soaked towel to the back of her head. "It's started to bleed again. I thought it had stopped."

The look of worry on the dark woman's face made Glenna want to panic again, but she pushed it away. No time for panic with work to be done.

She turned to Mary. "Fetch some more linens – towels, sheets, and whatever else you see that we might use." Glenna took off her apron, folded it up, and put it to the wound, letting the weight of Melanie's head against her hand apply pressure.

"Her horse went wild when it saw a snake and threw Melanie." The maid called her mistress Melanie? But now wasn't the time to question that.

"And she hit her head." Gemona stated the obvious. "On a rock. I was thrown, too, but I didn't get hurt other than a few bruises." The maid looked up, her eyes begging for reassurance. "Will she be all right?"

"I sent for the closest doctor. I'm sure she'll be just fine." If they could get this bleeding stopped, that is. And Glenna didn't like Melanie's pallor. They needed to stop this blood flow as soon as possible.

Mary came in with a stack of linens, and set them in the chair. Glenna picked up two large towels and handed one to Mary. "Wet this with that pitcher and basin and wring it out until it's just damp."

Mary scurried to do as she was told. "Help me turn her on her side more. That might help stop the bleeding, and it will make it easier for us to get to the wound." She looked up at Melanie's maid. "What's your name now?"

"Oh, sorry. I didn't think. It's Gemona."

"And I'm Glenna O'Brady, the housekeeper here."

Glenna worked for at least thirty minutes, applying fresh compresses and giving them to Mary to rinse out and have ready to use again. Gemona helped hold Melanie and assisted. The bleeding slowed but didn't completely stop. "If that doctor doesn't get here soon, I'm going to go downstairs and see what herbs I have that might stop the bleeding. In fact, I think I'll do that. Here, you take over with the cool compresses, Gemona. I should have some Shepherd's Purse, although I wish I had it fresh-picked. I'll send Miles word to look for some, but the best of them are likely gone now."

Glenna had just gotten downstairs, when she heard Dr. Winston at the door. After brief introductions she led him upstairs, telling him what she knew of the situation as they walked.

The doctor walked into the room and looked around. "Let me clear the room of everyone, except Miss Carter's maid."

Glenna and Mary left. This would be a good time to inform Lucas on what had happened. He was likely worried and anxious, but it almost served him right for staying sequestered in his office.

Lucas had his head in his hands when she walked in, but he jumped up. "How is she?"

"I'm afraid she's lost a lot of blood, and she's still unconscious. The doctor is with her now."

He turned almost as pale as Melanie had been and gripped the edge of his desk. "She's bleeding?"

"That's right, you didn't know she hit her head on a rock when she fell and has an ugly gash in the back of her head."

Lucas sat down and ran his hand through his dark hair. Then he looked up. "Why didn't you stay with her while the doctor examined her?"

"He wanted everyone to leave but Gemona, Melanie's maid. Are you going to see her?"

"I don't know." He didn't look at her. "I'm not sure she needs to wake up to see me there. I'm liable to scare her senseless with or without the mask."

"But you were going to see her in Winton."

"With a bandage on my face."

"I can put a bandage on you now if that would help." She couldn't understand why he hesitated to see Melanie.

He shook his head. "Now is not the time to think about me. We need to make sure Melanie is taken care of. She should be our priority."

Glenna could do both, but she didn't argue. She could tell Lucas was too distracted and worried right now.

Glenna heard the doctor descending the stairs. "Well, let me go see about Melanie."

Lucas nodded, his eyes filled with apprehension.

"The bleeding has completely stopped, at least for now," the distinguished looking man said. "I wouldn't be surprised if there's some more seepage along, however. You needn't be concerned unless it becomes constant or heavy. She needs to stay in bed, even if she gains consciousness."

"Do you expect her to wake up soon?"

"There's no way of telling. She could, or it might take a while. There have been cases where the patient never woke up, and in her weakened state, we could lose her; but I don't think that will happen. She's young and healthy, and those things are in her favor. Most cases I know of gained consciousness within two weeks, and I'll be more concerned if she doesn't."

"What should we be doing to help her?"

"Besides making sure she rests, try to get liquids into her, including broth to build her strength. If she does gain consciousness, make sure she stays calm and isn't upset."

"We'll need to contact her family."

"Talk with her maid. Only do so right away if they won't upset her in any way. If that's not the case, delay it as long as you can. In fact, if you will get me their address, I will write to them and give them this information."

"That would be good. I'll get the information from Gemona and send it over to your sister's. Thank you, doctor. You can send us your bill."

He waved that concern away. "We'll take care of that later. I'll be by tomorrow to check on her. In the meantime, if there's any change or if you need me, just let me know."

"How long will you be in the area, doctor?"

"I had planned to visit my sister for at least a month, but I can stay longer if needed."

Glenna nodded and trudged back to let Lucas know what the doctor had said. She wished she had better news to report, because nothing in this report would ease his mind.

Lucas went to his room with the pretense of retiring, but he knew he couldn't sleep. He sat in a chair to start with, his mind almost numb with worry but refusing to quieten.

How ironic to have Melanie under his roof but with her health in jeopardy. He'd prayed more today than he ever had in his life, but he felt no peace.

He tried to tell himself that worrying didn't help her or him, but he couldn't stop it. He couldn't understand how he could care so much for a woman he'd only met once, but that didn't change the fact that he did.

He recognized that God was in control, and he should turn everything over to Him, but he wanted to help Melanie. He didn't like feeling so helpless. He shook himself. He needed to trust God. He knew God wanted the best for His children and needed to hold on to that promise.

"Lord, heal Melanie, I pray. And please help me in my weakness, help my unbelief and uncertainties, and help me to trust Thee totally." His mumbled prayer joined the barrage of others, and there would be many more to follow.

After he knew that Glenna had gone to bed and likely to sleep, he paced. Although he felt weak and drained, he also felt so nervous, he couldn't relax, and movement helped a little.

When his body tired of that, he lay down on his bed but didn't undress. Finally, he put on his mask, just in case, and slipped down the hall to stand in front of Melanie's room. He listened intently, but heard nothing. He lowered his head and said a quick, silent prayer that Melanie would recover quickly and that he could do this without repercussions.

Knowing he took a risk, he methodically opened the door, making as little noise as possible. He eased into the room, glad he had come in his stocking feet, which would be quieter.

With no light in the room, he had to get close to the bed before he could see her, but the bit of moonlight filtering in the window helped. He looked around and saw a cot pushed against the wall on the far side of the room with a hump on it he assumed to be Gemona, Melanie's maid.

Then he bent over Melanie and gave her his total attention. She lay on her side facing him, so lovely with her hair spreading over the pillow. He moved even closer to see the back of her head. A portion of hair had been cut away, and a bandage covered the wound so he couldn't tell how it looked or anything about the knot he imagined to be there.

She looked so pale. He wanted to run his hand down her cheek and feel its softness, but he didn't dare do so. He didn't want to do anything that could be construed as ungentlemanly. The wry smile came when he realized entering a lady's bed chamber could be viewed as exactly that.

After a few minutes, he picked up a chair and placed it closer to the bed, sat down, and picked up her hand when a weak moan slipped from her lips. He would allow himself to touch her hand and hoped beyond reason it might comfort her in some way.

Strange, he didn't feel as agitated sitting here beside her, holding her hand. And, although the situation hadn't changed, he didn't feel as anxious.

He must have sat there for a couple of hours when he forced himself to get up. The danger of Gemona getting up to check on her mistress increased with every minute he remained.

He placed the chair back where it had been, and eased away with the same caution he had entered. When he finally closed the door, he bowed his head and said another prayer for Melanie, this one not as hurried.

When he got back to his room, he quickly undressed. He would go to bed and perhaps he could get to sleep before his fears and nervousness returned. Just before putting out the light he glanced at the clock. Three o'clock, later than he thought. He had been in Melanie's room for over three hours.

Chapter Sixteen: Pretense

"What! This is completely unacceptable!" Jenkins hurled the words at William, his face hard with resolve. "Go get her and bring her home right now!" William had never seen the man so angry.

"We need to do what's best for Melanie." William tried to reason with the man. "The doctor said we should stay away until she's recovered enough to be moved. At least we know her whereabouts now." That should be a relief after searching for her so diligently but finding no sign of her.

"Nonsense! I don't believe it!" The man's voice almost reverberated in William's ears and he felt the beginnings of a headache. He did wish Jenkins would lower his voice. "This is just some ploy to get out of marrying me!"

"Why would Melanie want to do that?" Although he could pretty well answer his own question right now with the way Lott had reacted. If it had been Constance,

William would have been more concerned about her welfare than anything else.

Jenkins snorted. "Where have you been hiding? Surely you recognize marrying me is not what your sister wanted, but I won't be thwarted. I will have Melanie if I have to find someone to marry us with her unconscious. At least she won't be able to fight against me then."

William didn't dare examine that uncouth statement too closely. He didn't want to know what the man meant. "That wouldn't be legal."

Jenkins blew out another heavy breath, sounding more like an angry bull. "You're probably right, but I'm going to find her and see for myself how she fares. If the doctor is exaggerating, we might still be able to hold the wedding on the appointed date."

"I don't think that's a good idea. For one thing, the doctor didn't say where Melanie was, just that we would be contacted when she recovers enough to see us. But more importantly, he emphasized that any upheaval or conflict could be detrimental to her mental well-being. I'll not have you rushing in and upsetting her." William stopped just short of forbidding Jenkins to see Melanie, because he feared that would only increase his ire.

Jenkins sucked in a deep breath. "I'm going to track her down, and then I'll decide if I should step in or not. Think about it William. She goes missing, we can't find her, and no one saw her after your slave left her and her maid at the river. And fishing is another thing she had no business doing, by the way. She may be someone's captive for all we know. They could be abusing her as we speak. And, no matter what you say, I still think young Askew has something to do with her disappearance."

"I've known the Askews all my life, and Toby's father told me his son had left on some business well before Melanie disappeared. He wouldn't lie. I'm certain of that."

"Yes, but the man didn't know what kind of business, and that doesn't sound logical to me."

"Toby is a grown man and, as such, his affairs are his own. I'm sure he will clear it all up once he gets home."

"Let me know when that is. In the meantime, I'm going to find out where Melanie is."

William noticed Jenkins didn't bother to say "Miss Carter" as he usually did, but William chose not to address that matter either. "You let me know if you find Melanie. If you decide to put in an appearance, I insist on accompanying you."

Jenkins gave him a cutting look but said nothing. William sure hoped the man didn't rush in and make a mess of it all, harming Melanie in the process. Perhaps he should track down the doctor and at least give him warning.

Blast it all! William wanted to know how Melanie fared, too, but he'd put her interests above his own. Maybe he had been too hasty in deciding Jenkins would be a perfect husband for his sister. Scenes of Melanie pleading with him to not force her into this union flashed in his mind.

It would be extremely difficult to back out of the commitment now, but not totally impossible. Perhaps they could say that marriage would be too much for her delicate condition to handle following the accident and at least postpone the wedding for a time until he could observe Jenkins more closely and reassess the situation.

He would try to do what was best for Mel. Her accident had reminded him of how much she meant to him. Surely he could think of a way to handle his financial situation without Jenkins if that's what he needed to do.

He shook his head. He'd go check on Constance and the baby and maybe that would alleviate his uneasiness. He smiled at the thought of his little girl. Mel would be thrilled to learn of her niece, now a few days old. He wished she'd been here for the birth.

William saw Jenkins at church the following Sunday, surprising since the man hadn't attended since Melanie had been gone. It didn't take him long to realize Jenkins came to ask around for any information that might lead him to Melanie.

William wondered why he hadn't already discovered where she'd been taken. If nothing else, Jenkins had the persistence and determination to uncover any information he wanted. William didn't know if the fact Jenkins hadn't done so made him happy or worried. He didn't want Jenkins to go against the doctor's instructions; but if he couldn't find Melanie, she must be well-hidden indeed. That gave him a foreboding that Jenkins might just be right. This whole affair might be more sinister than it appeared, and he had no idea what to do about it.

Gemona heard the faintest sound and knew the man, who must be Lucas, had come again. Each night now he came and sat beside Melanie's bed for several hours.

The first time she saw him, she almost cried out, but something told her he meant no harm. Time had proven that to be true, but she couldn't imagine why the man would sneak into the room at night. Why didn't he just come during the day to check on her?

She tried to see what he looked like, but he never lit the lamp, and she couldn't make out any features from her cot across the room. Something about his head didn't look right, but she couldn't see clearly enough to tell much about it.

She thought he usually held Melanie's hand for a time, but she would need to sit up and maybe move closer to know for sure. Once he seemed to reach for something on her pillow, but he hadn't done that again.

Gemona closed her eyes. She usually drifted back off to sleep before the man left. Sometimes his leaving would wake her and sometimes not. She didn't always wake up when he came in, but she'd seen him often enough she felt sure he came every night.

She'd watched him and Melanie in the Garden in Edenton. Even from a distance, she could feel their attraction to each other, and Melanie had later confirmed it. By the tender way he sat beside her bed now, she knew he'd be better for her than Lott Jenkins, and since she wouldn't consider marrying Toby, this would be the best solution. Now if Melanie would only fully recover.

Tears slid down Gemona's cheeks in the dark, and she dared not wipe them away with Lucas in the room. She had heard the doctor say he'd be concerned if Melanie didn't wake up within two weeks, and two weeks would soon be up.

Between her and Glenna, they'd managed to spoon some broth and some water into Melanie, but it wasn't enough. If she didn't rouse enough to drink more, things could become dire indeed. She just had to get well. Gemona would never forgive herself if she didn't. She went back to sleep praying for Melanie to get better and asking the Good Lord to forgive her for any wrong she'd done.

When Glenna came to check on Melanie the next morning, Gemona realized that she'd never asked about

Lucas. She'd better do that or it would seem odd. "Who owns this place?"

"He's a private man who keeps to himself." The housekeeper didn't turn to look at Gemona.

"Will we not meet him?"

"I think Melanie may when she's up to it."

Gemona didn't know why the answer that sounded like a slight surprised her. As a slave, she'd grown up being ignored or treated as insignificant. Only Melanie didn't treat her that way. She looked at her friend in the bed. *Oh, please get well.*

Two days later, Gemona sat trying to spoon some milk into Melanie for breakfast. She'd propped the invalid's head up with pillows, but she still had to take care that Melanie didn't strangle.

After the long, boring procedure, she went to lay Melanie back down when her eyelids quivered. "Melanie? Melanie, wake up."

Her eyes opened.

"Oh, praise God. How do you feel?" Gemona felt like dancing with joy.

"Weak." Her voice sounded it. "What happened? I remember falling off my horse."

Gemona gave her a condensed version of what had happened since then, but she omitted any mention of Lucas for now. The doctor didn't want her upset or excited

"Has my family been notified? Have they been to see me?"

"The doctor sent them word but recommended that they wait to visit. He said you shouldn't be upset until you're better healed, and I'm glad. That means Lott hasn't come either."

"I'm so tired, I can't seem to keep my eyes open."

"Please listen to me before you go back to sleep. This is important. The sooner they know you are all right, the sooner Lott will be here. You need to pretend that you're still unconscious when anyone but me is about."

"Pretend?" Melanie started to shake her head, but she winced, and Gemona knew the movement had hurt too much.

"You haven't listened to me on anything else to do with avoiding marriage to Lott, but listen to me now. At least do this until you're strong enough for us to talk about it."

Melanie had drifted back off to sleep. Gemona just hoped she'd heard the advice and would follow it.

Melanie woke up with a dull ache making opening her eyes or moving difficult. She opened her eyes anyway and remembered Gemona telling her they were in the home of someone who had seen to their care.

Gemona came closer to the bed and smiled. "I'm glad you're finally awake again. Glenna, the housekeeper here just brought you some chicken broth for supper. We need to get more nourishment in you if you're going to get your strength back."

With Gemona's help, she sat up some in the bed, although she had to lean heavily against the pillows Gemona placed between her and the head of the bed. She found herself too weak to hold and drink the small bowl of broth, but Gemona helped her steady it.

She drank most of the liquid, and Gemona looked pleased. "That worked much better than me trying to spoon it into you and make sure you swallowed it."

Gemona wanted her to drink a glass of water, too, but she felt so full from the broth she could only manage a few sips.

"About this pretending…."

A knock interrupted, and Gemona moved to open the door after glancing back at Melanie with an admonishing glare that begged her to play along.

Melanie closed her eyes, still not wanting to pretend she hadn't regained consciousness, but needing to talk with Gemona about it first. The maid might have some other piece of pertinent information to share.

"Come in Dr. Winston," she heard Gemona say.

"How's our patient doing today?"

"Just a little better, I think. I got more broth into her than usual for dinner."

"Good, good. Any progress is better than none." He proceeded to pick up Melanie's arm, but she remained limp. He lifted each eyelid while peering into her face. "I do think she seems a bit more alert. I'll check on her again in two days. By then I hope to see even more progress. Once she comes to, I expect she'll recover quickly."

"You don't think there'll be any lasting damage?" Gemona was almost too skilled in deception.

"One can never be sure, but I hope not. She's young, healthy, and strong, at least before the accident, so I don't think there'll be lasting problems."

"I need to tell you something so you won't be frightened." Gemona said after the doctor left. "A man often comes in and sits by your bed at night. He might hold your hand, but he never does anything more."

It sounded too improper and odd to imagine. Melanie's alarm must have shown on her face.

"Don't worry. I think it might be Lucas."

Melanie couldn't imagine that either. "What makes you think so?"

"Well, uh, I did watch the two of you in Edenton and he has to live somewhere in the area to have been invited to the masquerade ball. Besides, the figure looks to be the right size and moves about as Lucas did."

"But you aren't sure?"

"I haven't seen him clearly in the dark room if that's what you're asking. But it's the only thing that makes sense. Who else would be likely to come in and tenderly sit with you for hours?"

"I think you may be seeing what you want to see. Why would he just come in at night? Why not come in the day and make himself known?"

"That's a good question, and one I don't have the answer to. But I'm glad to see you're as bright as ever. Hitting your head when you fell hasn't affected your mind at all. Now, you go to sleep. I know you must be tired, and if you wake up tonight with a man beside your bed, you can see what you think. Just don't let him know that you're awake."

Melanie did feel exhausted. But she didn't know about pretending she hadn't regained consciousness, especially if this turned out to be Lucas. She just hoped she would wake up if he came again. The way she felt right now, she might not.

Melanie awoke when she heard the door slowly open, perhaps because she'd been listening for any sound as she drifted in and out of sleep. The moon must be small tonight or the sky partly cloudy, because the tiniest amount of light came in the window, leaving the room in near darkness. She could see little of the man as he stealthily moved a chair beside her bed and sat down. His soft sigh sounded forlorn and miserable, and her heart went out to him. If this was Lucas, maybe he did care for her, too.

She didn't think that he could see enough to tell her eyes were open, but if he did, she wouldn't mind. She hadn't decided if she would go along with Gemona's subterfuge or not, and she wouldn't if this turned out to be Lucas.

She could see just his outline, a little darker than the charcoal of the room. The breadth of his shoulders and his form fit the man she'd met in the Edenton garden.

He gently picked up her hand, and her heart raced as his thumb stroked it with a touch as light as a feather. She felt sure this was Lucas, but something about his head didn't look right. Was he wearing a strange hat? But then his neck also looked much too thick. "Lucas?"

He froze.

"Is it you?"

She thought he wasn't going to answer, but he eventually did. "You're conscious. I'm so glad. My prayers have been answered." His soft whisper sounded much as he had that night in Edenton.

"I have so many questions."

"I'm sure you do, but now that you're awake, I need to get out of your room. I'll come back in the morning, and we can talk then." He started to bring her hand to his mouth, but must have thought better of it, because he had it halfway up when he carefully placed it back on the bed.

"You heard?" she asked Gemona when Lucas had gone.

"I did." The maid got up and came to stand beside the bed. Melanie could hear the pleasure and excitement in the slave's voice. "I knew that had to be him. But I'm not sure you did the right thing in speaking to him and letting him know you had awakened." The pleasure had left Gemona's voice.

"I'm not about to try to deceive Lucas, and he's not likely to turn me over to Lott if I ask him not to."

"Well, you try to get back to sleep now. You'll want to be fresh and strong when Lucas comes back tomorrow."

But Melanie found herself too excited to get back to sleep. What were the chances that Toby Askew would kidnap her and she'd have an accident escaping only to end up with Lucas? This had to be of God. This had to be the miracle she'd prayed for.

Chapter Seventeen: Disguised

Lucas went back to his room in a daze. What were the chances that Melanie would wake up with him in the room and then recognize him immediately? His heart wanted to jump for joy that she had done so, because she had to have been thinking of him some since the ball. But this would greatly complicate everything. He jerked off his mask. At least he knew she hadn't seen his scars.

He rubbed his hand through his hair and then put his face in his hands. He thought about letting Melanie see him as he was so he'd know right away if he had a chance with her, but he discarded that idea. No, it would be better to insure she'd returned to full health first. The doctor had told Glenna that she should be kept calm after she woke up.

He didn't understand why his presence in her room hadn't appeared to upset her. Most women would have been terrified to see a man in her bedroom, but then Melanie had recognized him. That she must trust him a great deal pleased him to no end. He could see so many miracles playing out before him. Did he dare hope for the miracle that she would accept him, scars and all?

Well, he needed to get to bed and get some sleep. He wanted to be ready to see Melanie as soon as possible, and he wanted to look his best. He laughed aloud. As if he'd ever look good enough to impress anyone.

"I think you're making a mistake." Glenna had brought the bandaging supplies into his office as he requested.

"When do you not?"

She proceeded to bandage his face, not an easy task since she declared she wanted to leave his unscarred side free of the bandage. Lucas agreed that would be best. If his whole face were covered, it would look scary indeed.

"It would be better if you let her see all of who you are at the very start, and didn't try to deceive her."

"How do you know that would be better? Besides, I'm not trying to deceive her. I just don't want to upset her and cause her to have a relapse." Even he recognized the half-truth there.

"Covering your face so she won't know you have scars isn't deceiving her?"

"Has she had breakfast?" He wanted to change the subject.

"Yes. I think she's more excited than you are."

Lucas didn't doubt that, because he didn't know if he felt excitement at all. Nervousness and fear overshadowed any anticipation, but he did look forward to talking with her. He just wished he could wear his costume again or at least his mask.

"There." Glenna stepped back and looked at her work. "That's the best I can do."

He stood and started for the stairs. He found himself both eager and dreading the coming encounter. Before he knocked on Melanie's door, he went to his room and looked in the mirror, something he rarely did if he could help it.

Glenna had done a decent job with the bandage, but it still appeared bulky and horrible to him. Well, it looked better than his disfigured face, for sure.

He tapped on the door, and the maid opened it. It seemed strange not to slip in without making a sound.

Melanie's bright smile dropped as soon as she saw his bandages. "Are you injured?"

He nodded. He was, but it had happened years ago.

"Is it painful?" Concern permeated her voice.

"Not any longer, but I'm afraid there will be scars."

"I'm just glad you're all right. Now I know why your image looked odd last night in the dark." She frowned. "Although the outline still doesn't seem quite the same, but please sit down." She indicated the chair he usually occupied that had already been pulled forward.

"How are you this morning?" He wanted to talk about her and not him.

"Better. At least I'm awake." Her teasing grin made him smile, too.

"I need to see Glenna about something." Gemona started to leave the room. "I'll just leave the door open for propriety's sake, and I'll be back shortly."

Melanie must have seen the question on his face. "I asked her to give us a little privacy to talk if she could."

Her direct stare made Lucas glad he had the bandage over his scars. "You're even more handsome than I imagined." Her bold statement made her blush, and he found her embarrassment endearing.

He regretted her statement, knowing she'd think him ugly, even grotesque, when she saw the rest of his face, but he liked it that she'd been thinking about him. "Tell me what happened to get you here. Your maid told Glenna some, but I'd like to hear it from your point of view, because I think you'll give more details."

She began to tell him what had happened.

"Wait! You were kidnapped?" Lucas stopped her to clarify. That someone would dare kidnap her raised his ire.

"Yes, and the kidnapper turned out to be Toby Askew, one of my best friends. We grew up together. I'm telling you this in confidence, because I don't want to get Toby in trouble. He did it to keep me from marrying Lott Jenkins."

"Did Askew plan to marry you himself?"

"He would have, but I refused. Toby is a great guy, and he deserves someone who loves him like a wife should love a husband. I couldn't do that."

"Even if it meant marrying someone you thought less of?"

"Even then. I decided to trust God. I didn't believe He wanted me to marry Lott, and I kept expecting a miracle."

"Your faith is stronger than mine." He looked at her in awe, realizing how she thought almost completely opposite of Margaret Ann.

"Did you not fear your reputation would suffer after being kidnapped?"

"I did, but Toby thought Gemona's presence would be enough. However, I'm still not happy with him, and I can't help but wonder if there's not something else to his reasoning."

"Did he treat you well through the kidnapping?"

"He did, although it was rather scary before I knew it was him." She continued to tell about how they had left Winton and camped out for the night, how she and Gemona escaped, and about her horse throwing her. He knew what had happened after that.

"I've been so worried about you," he told her when she'd finished her tale. "Do I need to inform your family that you're conscious?" Lucas dreaded the thoughts of her family coming to take her away, but he wanted to do the right thing.

"What's the date?"

"June the twelfth."

"That late? Then yes." She smiled. "I've already missed my wedding."

"This is Saturday. I'll take care of it first thing Monday morning." That would give him two extra days with her. "I can see you're tiring, and you need to take special care that you don't overdo. I'll leave you to rest for now, but I'd like to visit with you again this afternoon if you think you'll feel up to it."

"I would like that. It's so good to see you again. I've thought of you often since our time in the garden in Edenton."

"And I of you."

"But I don't understand why you just came in to see me at night."

He started to use his injuries as an excuse, but he realized that would make little sense. If he felt like coming in at night, he could have come during the day. Would saying he'd been occupied with other things be too much of a lie? Probably. "I didn't want you to wake up and see my head practically covered and be frightened back into unconsciousness. I figured the dark would help disguise me." That should be close enough to the truth.

He stood and did something he'd wanted to do every night but hadn't because of his mask. He picked up her hand and kissed it. "Until this afternoon then. You get some sleep."

"What are you doing?" Glenna came into his office without knocking like usual. He'd allowed the woman too many liberties, but he had no other family. He and his brother in England were now estranged.

"I've just finished writing to Melanie's brother telling him she's conscious and doing much better if he wants to see her."

"Did you tell him the doctor still advises her not to travel yet, although the family is welcome to visit her?"

"Yes, I did." She should know that he'd want to impart that information. The longer Melanie could stay here, the better. He'd also said only the immediate family should come for now. He hoped that would deter Jenkins, but he had his doubts.

"When are you going to take off that bandage?"

He wanted to tell her not until Melanie left. They'd had a wonderful two days with him visiting her in the mornings and again in the afternoons. His respect, admiration, and love for the woman grew with each visit. *Love*? Could it really be love this soon? He didn't know for sure, but he knew this went far beyond anything he'd felt for Margaret Ann, and he thought he'd been in love with her.

"Melanie is going to come downstairs today, so this would be a perfect time to remove your bandages. You'll never know for sure what her reaction will be until you do."

He wanted to tell her no time would be perfect for that. "I don't think so today, but I'll think about doing it before her brother comes."

"It had better be soon, because I've got a feeling her brother and perhaps his wife will come quickly once they receive that letter. Winton and Colerain are not all that far apart."

"I can't understand why I can't find her!" Jenkins paced the parlor too agitated to sit down.

William didn't even understand why Jenkins was here. He'd told him he'd heard no further word about Melanie.

"I can't believe she missed our wedding." The man continued his tirade. "All our plans thrown right out the window."

"I don't believe that was her choice."

"I'm not so sure." Jenkins stopped his pacing long enough to look at William. "And I think you need to help me find her. We could at least learn why she left from that slave of hers. Since Askew came home without her, I think she ran away."

"I assure you, if Melanie had run away, she would have taken Jericho with her. He's about as devoted to her welfare as Gemona is."

"I don't understand why you aren't more worried." William didn't appreciate his accusatory tone.

"I am concerned, and I pray for her several times a day, but I want to do what's best for Melanie. The doctor said we needed to wait until she'd recovered to see her and that she's too fragile to be moved now."

"And you believe him? The whole thing could be just a ruse. How do you know that letter came from a doctor? Anyone could have written it. Why, Melanie could be in danger as we speak."

"You don't trust anyone, do you?"

"No, I don't, and that's what's got me where I am today."

William heard a knock on the door, and Shadrack led two men in. "This is Mr. Lassiter and Mr. Creighton, the sheriff from Edenton and his deputy."

William stood, greeted them, and introduced Jenkins. "What can I do for you, gentlemen?"

"We have a warrant for the arrest of Lott Jenkins on the charges of fraud and extortion." The men proceeded to secure Jenkins who had turned deathly pale.

"This is preposterous! You'll regret this. I'll sue for defamation of character." The volume of his protests faded as the men led him away."

William sat back stunned. Had Jenkins really just been arrested for unscrupulous business practices? He had never thought the man capable of this. But then again, the side of Jenkins he'd seen since Melanie had disappeared didn't make it that incredible.

He got up and went to give Constance the news. He liked to drop in and see his daughter at breaks during the day anyway.

"A letter for you from a Mr. Lucas Hall." Shadrack brought the missive in on a silver tray. William shook his head. Constance and her efforts to be the royalty of Hertford County, but he indulged her. He opened and read the letter:

Dear Mr. Carter:

It is with great pleasure that I write to inform you that your sister is awake, and the doctor says her immediate family are welcome to come visit her and see for themselves how she's doing, but she still isn't strong enough to travel. She lost a lot of blood when she fell from her horse and gashed her head on a rock, and her attendants haven't been able to feed her much until she awoke. I have great hopes that she will improve quickly now that has happened.

Don't feel you need to rush to her side. Dr. Winston, my housekeeper, the staff here, and Gemona are seeing that she receives the best of care. We are glad to have her with us, and she may remain as long as she desires.

Although you and your wife are more than welcome to visit and even spend some time with us, if

you'd like, the doctor doesn't want others visiting until
she regains some of her strength.

 I hope this eases your mind, as it has mine. I have
been concerned about her condition but better now that
prayers have been answered. I live a rather secluded
life, near Colerain, but I will inform my staff to be
expecting you and allow you immediate entrance. I have
enclosed a map I drew to help you find us.

 Respectfully yours,
 Lucas Hall
 The Marquess of Dorset

William read the closing again. A marquess! Of
course it officially meant nothing in this country, but it
would still give him status. Constance would certainly
be impressed. He hurried to show her and make
arrangements to travel to Colerain.

Melanie snuggled into Lucas as he carried her
down the stairs. He had insisted he do it himself rather
than leave it to a servant, and she'd agreed, because she
preferred that he did it. With her arms around his neck
and her head against his chest, her heart beat about as
erratically as a small boat at sea in a hurricane. But she
loved the feel of his strong arms around her.

He might have been her fantasy knight before, but the reality of the man surpassed her dreams. They had spent hours together just talking, and he never seemed to tire of her, always listened to what she had to say, and gave her more respect than anyone had in a long time.

Even after he left her, she could see his thick hair, such a dark brown it appeared to be black. And those eyes were so expressive, reminding Melanie of the bright blue of a shallow sea or the deepest tint of the sky. But his face, or the left side of it she could see, is what took her breath away. She had never seen such a handsome man. She couldn't even describe it.

She knew Lucas had sent William a letter, but she hoped her brother would take his time in coming. Although the doctor had said she shouldn't be moved yet, she couldn't be sure what William would do, and Lott could come, too, regardless what anyone said. Her fiancé did what he wanted without listening to anyone else.

Her fiancé. She hated the thought, but at least he wasn't her husband. Yet. But now that she'd gotten to know Lucas better, marrying Lott, or anyone else, felt inconceivable. *Oh Lord, please let me end up with Lucas, because I'm falling madly in love with him.*

"Here you go." Lucas placed her gently on the sofa in a small sitting room. She would have much preferred to stay in his arms. "Thank you."

Gemona made sure her pillows were adjusted and her skirts arranged. She wanted to also cover her with a sheet, but Melanie refused. With all her skirts, stays, and under things on again, she already felt too warm, and Lucas carrying her downstairs had only added to a rise in temperature.

She wore her one dress, but it had been washed and ironed. Glenna was having two others made for her, but she hadn't needed to dress before now.

Lucas pulled a chair close to the sofa, and Gemona took a seat across the room but in view. She would still likely hear whatever they said in the small, intimate room.

Lucas leaned toward her. "Do you think your brother will come quickly and do you think Mr. Jenkins will accompany him?"

"More than likely. William will come as quickly as he can. I'm rather surprised he listened to the doctor and didn't try to come at once. Lott's headstrong enough to do what he wants regardless of what anyone tells him."

Lucas clenched his jaws before answering. "Lott Jenkins won't get past me and my staff. I will promise you that. You don't have to fear him while you're here under my care, and I plan to have a talk with your brother about the man."

Melanie wanted to ask him exactly what he meant, but he continued with his questions. "Do think William will stay overnight or longer? I did give him that invitation."

"If Constance comes, he might. But she may have already had the baby, and that might change things."

"Tell me about your brother's holdings." Lucas always kept the conversation going.

"We live in one of the larger homes in Winton. The plantation house out in the country where I grew up burned down, and William never rebuilt it, because Constance prefers to live in town. William still farms the land, however. He has an overseer and about forty to fifty slaves."

He raised his eyebrows. "And I'm guessing you also have slaves in the house in town and Gemona is also a slave."

"Yes, there're about a dozen house slaves counting the ones who take care of the grounds and stable." She looked at her maid. "Gemona is a slave, but I think of her as a maid and my friend. When William asked me what I wanted him to give me for a wedding present, I told him Gemona. I want him to free her, although she may choose to stay with me. We've become close."

He looked thoughtful. "There are some movements in England working to abolish slavery there. I think we may have a good chance of doing away with the slave trade soon."

"We?"

"I'm one of the ones opposed to slavery. Does that upset you?"

"Not in the least. I would be in total agreement, but you won't find many others in this area who would. In fact, I helped get a cruel overseer on William's plantation replaced with Toby Askew's older brother, who will be much better. But does that mean you don't own slaves?"

"It does. All my help are paid servants."

Lucas must have recognized how tired she'd grown. The dressing to come downstairs had worn her out. "Let me let you rest for a while, and I'll have dinner with you if you'll allow it. Are you comfortable enough?" He stood.

"I'm comfortable, and I'll look forward to seeing you at dinner." She snuggled deeper into the sofa, hoping to dream of her handsome knight. Or had he turned into her Prince Charming?

Chapter Eighteen: Revelations

The next morning, Melanie made her way downstairs with Gemona by her side to steady her. As much as she would have loved to have Lucas carry her down again, she refused to pretend with him, and she did feel stronger this morning.

Lucas must have been listening for her, because he met her halfway down and held to her other side. He helped her to the sofa, and she sat upright this time. "Are you all right?"

She smiled up at him. "I'm doing much better this morning."

"May I?" He indicated sitting beside her on the sofa.

Her smile widened. "Please. Have a seat."

"I'm guessing your brother will be here sometime today." He didn't sound pleased.

She wanted to see her family and learn if she had a niece or nephew, but she hoped they didn't want her to leave right away. She would miss Lucas.

Instead of continuing the conversation, Lucas sat silently by her side, fumbling with something in his pocket.

"You're being unusually quiet this morning." She reached over and patted his hand. "Is something wrong?"

He immediately took her hand in his. "No, but Glenna tells me it's time to remove my bandages."

"I would think you'd be glad to be rid of them."

He looked down at their hands. "What if I'm badly scarred?"

"I'm afraid I don't understand the question. I would hate it for your sake, but it wouldn't change anything, would it?"

He looked at her as if he didn't believe her. "Do you think you can stand to see me if I'm grossly disfigured?"

She squeezed his hand for reassurance. He'd always seemed so strong and confident to her, but now he appeared scared and vulnerable. "I would love you all the more." She could have crawled under the sofa. Had she just told him she loved him? A lady wouldn't do that before the man professed his love first.

"Oh, darling, I hope you meant that."

Why was he so insecure and doubtful? This just didn't make any sense.

"Melanie, I need to explain something. These aren't new scars, but I've had them for a few years. A cannon blew up beside me in a military training exercise. It killed two men and left three of us maimed."

Melanie tried to understand. Why had he not told her all this to begin with?

"I was engaged at the time."

Melanie's breath almost left her. Lucas must have felt her tense, for he laced his fingers through hers, but he continued. "Margaret Ann ran away in disgust, and she made sure she never had to confront me again."

Now she was beginning to understand, but surely he didn't think Melanie would react that way. "Then she must have never loved you."

"That's what Glenna says, but it gets worse. My older brother inherited my father's title of Duke, but he had married. Less than a year after I came home from the military, he died from a hunting accident, and Charles, my middle brother, inherited the dukedom since Alfred didn't leave any children. Three months later he and Margaret Ann were married. Charles gave me the family's lands in America to get rid of me, and I've been here ever since."

"And he's become a hermit here," Glenna added. Melanie hadn't heard her come up.

Lucas dropped Melanie's hand, pulled a pair of scissors from his pocket, and handed them to Glenna. His face had become like stone. "Since you are here, you can do the honors."

The housekeeper took the scissors without speaking, snipped the edge of a bandage, and began unwrapping it. Lucas closed his eyes as if he couldn't bear to see Melanie's reaction. When Glenna got near the end, she gave a brief pause, and then ripped the rest away.

Melanie sucked in her breath but took care not to gasp. The scars were ugly and ridged, stretching over crinkled skin. They ran down the right side of his face, just missing his eye and ending in a U-shape at the bottom of his jaw.

Without looking at her, he took off his gloves showing his right hand enveloped in scars. "The right side of my body is similar."

She moved over toward him and ran her hand down his right cheek. "You're still the most handsome man I've ever seen."

His eyes flew to hers and searched them for any deceit. "Are you sure?"

He looked so excited and eager, she couldn't help but laugh. "Absolutely positive."

"Oh, darling." He pulled her into his arms. "I didn't dare hope."

"I knew it!" Glenna screamed. "I just knew she'd be different."

She lay her head on his shoulder, and wished she could stay in his arms, but it would all be over too soon. Tears trickled from her eyes at the thought.

He must have sensed her change in moods, because he pulled back. "What's wrong? Are you reconsidering?"

She shook her head. "No, but I'm engaged to Lott. He'll never let me go."

"Didn't you tell me in Edenton that Jenkins's money influenced your brother in his favor?"

"Yes?" She didn't see how that had to do with anything.

"Honey, I'm sure I have many times over Jenkins's wealth. Surely we can persuade William to change his mind."

"Do you think so?" Oh, how she hoped he was right.

"I do. As long as your family doesn't reject me because of these hideous scars, I think we have a good chance of swaying them."

She took his right hand and squeezed it. "Will you please quit referring to yourself so negatively? Your scars don't define who you are."

"Amen to that." Glenna interrupted again.

Lucas turned to his housekeeper. "Don't you and Gemona have something you could be doing, at least for a few minutes?"

Glenna stuck her head back and sniffed, but her eyes danced in joy. "I get the message. Come on Gemona. Let's go see how cook is coming along with dinner."

"Melanie, I want to ask William's permission to court you if you approve."

"Oh, I definitely approve, but what are your intentions?"

He looked at her carefully. "Are you teasing?"

"Not entirely."

"With the intention of marrying you, of course. Isn't that why couples are supposed to court?" As if he realized he'd forgot something important, he continued. "I love you, Melanie. I don't know how it happened so fast, but it did. I want to spend the rest of my life with you as my wife, have children with you, and grow old with you. You already have my heart; I just want to give you time so that you can love me and give me your heart, too."

"I already have."

He acted as if he didn't hear her or couldn't believe it. "Are you sure?"

She nodded and laughed again. "You're going to have to quit asking me that, or I'll think you don't trust me."

"Are you saying that you're ready to marry me?"

Again she nodded. "The sooner, the better." She felt her cheeks grow flushed at her brashness.

"Let's talk to your brother first, but if he's agreeable, you can expect a proposal very soon. And, darling, don't ever be embarrassed around me. I love it when you speak your mind."

"I'm almost looking forward to William coming now."

"Almost?"

"I'm still anxious about what Lott will do." She worried her bottom lip with her top teeth

"But if William gives us his permission, we can proceed with our plans. I think I can handle Lott."

"I hope you don't have to confront him. You don't know how devious, underhanded, and cruel he can be."

"Have some faith in me, and even more so, have faith in God."

"You're right. I trusted God to work a miracle, and He brought us together. I need to trust Him for its completion."

His beautiful blue eyes softened, "I want to kiss you so much right now, but I'll wait until we settle things with William, and I don't want to kiss someone else's fiancée. But soon, darling. Very soon."

At Lucas's insistence, Melanie started upstairs to lie down after dinner. She did grow tired quickly still.

"Would you like for me to carry you up the stairs?" he asked with a boyish grin on his face.

"I would like that very much, but I'm able to make it on my own, so I don't need you to carry me." She tried to tease him back.

But he scooped her up. "I'm here to see that you get what you want, my lady."

She couldn't help but laugh at his antics.

"I do believe the old Luke has emerged." Glenna called after him as he climbed the stairs.

"No, I think I'll turn out to be a hybrid of the two, but I still prefer to be called Lucas."

William found her in her bed about three o'clock. He rushed to her side. "How are you doing, Mel?"

"Very well. In fact, if you'll give me a few minutes, I'll join you in the parlor. I think we'll all be more comfortable there."

"If you're sure. I understand the doctor wants you to take it easy."

"He gave her permission to start staying up more, yesterday," Lucas told him. "If you'll follow me, we'll let Gemona get Melanie ready."

"How is Constance? Is the baby here?" She asked William before he left.

"Constance is fine, and you have a beautiful, little niece. We named her Nancy after Mama."

"That's good. I'll look forward to seeing her."

"And Constance had you a bag packed with some of your things for me to bring. I left it downstairs. You can have Gemona fetch it."

Melanie hurried to get ready, because she wanted to hear what William had to say. She held to the banister going down, but Gemona still stood close on the other side.

It sounded as if William and Lucas were talking about inconsequential things when she entered the parlor. She went to sit beside Lucas on the sofa, although she left plenty of space between them so William wouldn't frown.

"How is Lott?" It would be expected that she ask about him, and she wanted to know how he'd reacted to the news.

William cleared his throat and looked concerned. "About that. I hope you're not too fond of the man. The sheriff from Edenton arrested him for some unscrupulous business dealings done down there. Once news got out, other complaints were filed, and the man is in a ton of trouble."

"Really?" She looked at Lucas. "I knew he wasn't the man for me."

William looked embarrassed. "You did try to tell me, didn't you? I'm sorry I didn't listen. I promise I won't try to force anyone else on you against your will."

"Would you be so kind as to go find Glenna and tell her I'd like tea for three brought into the parlor?" Lucas looked at her, and she knew he wanted to speak to William.

"Of course." She hurried to do what he asked. She would like a cup of tea herself.

Glenna followed Melanie into the parlor carrying the tray with tea and cookies. The two men were laughing, and Melanie took that to be a good sign. William seemed to accept Lucas, scars and all. She resumed her seat beside Lucas.

"Shall I pour?" Glenna asked after sitting the tray on a table.

"Please," Lucas answered. "I don't want Melanie doing any more than she has to until she's fully recovered."

William looked at her. "Lucas asked me if he could court you. He tells me he wants to propose in the near future and that you approve of all this. Is that true? After the catastrophe with Jenkins, I don't want to go against your wishes again."

"Yes, I approve."

"Isn't this rather fast? There hasn't been any ungentlemanly behavior has there?"

"No, of course not. Lucas is a perfect gentleman, and this is not the first time we met."

"Oh?"

"We met at the masquerade ball in Edenton and talked for a while." Melanie knew William would assume they had been formally introduced.

"Did you dance with him?"

"Only once." Since William knew Lott had told her not to dance with any man more than once, that answer should suffice.

"And she enchanted me from that moment on." Lucas added.

"Very well. Is there anything else I need to know, Mel? I should probably be heading for home."

"You only have about three or four hours of daylight left. Don't you want to spend the night with us and get an early start in the morning?"

"I think I can make it home before dark since I rode my horse instead of bringing a carriage. To tell you the truth I want to get home and see my daughter. I've missed her and Constance this afternoon."

"I think I understand." Lucas looked at Melanie.

"You take good care of my sister." William shook Lucas's hand. "I wouldn't leave her if not for Gemona. That woman is tenacious in taking care of Melanie. And I do appreciate all you've done so far."

"Don't worry about anything. She's precious to me, and I will protect her from any harm."

Some sort of understanding seemed to pass between the two men. "I'll plan to return in ten days with the intention of taking Melanie home. Constance may want to come with me. If you need me before then, however, you'll know where to find me."

Lucas nodded, and William headed for the stable. Lucas put his hand on her back and led her to the sitting room she preferred. "You haven't become too tired have you? It's been a busy day."

"Yes, it has, but also a very satisfying day. My handsome knight has declared his love for me, my brother approves of him, and the villain that thought he would force me to marry him has been arrested. God has blessed.

"Indeed He has. And now for that kiss."

Chapter Nineteen: More Than a Kiss

Lucas felt as if he were living in a fantasy world where his dreams were coming true, but if so, he hoped he never had to leave it. The day's events had been extraordinary, but how could he be so dazed and so thrilled at the same time?

He pulled Melanie to her feet. He didn't want anything about their first kiss to be awkward, and remaining seated could make it that way. If he were to follow social codes to the letter, he wouldn't kiss her until they were engaged, but William had given him permission to court her with the understanding that he planned to propose, so he'd consider that good enough.

He took her in his arms, reveling at how well she fit. When his lips met hers, he'd never tasted anything so sweet, so moving, so enticing. But those were his last thoughts. Everything escaped his mind except the woman in his arms. In that moment, he lived and breathed Melanie, as if his soul also engulfed hers in a life-changing embrace.

When she opened her mouth and began to kiss him back, his body responded in ways he didn't think possible. The desire and need for her became so intense he pulled away before he lost all control.

But he stood holding her, surprised that he had enough strength to remain standing. With her head nestled on his chest, his heart only slowed a little. Could she hear it?

"I think our hearts are beating together," she whispered, as if she could read his thoughts.

Did he feel a dampness under her face? Was she crying? Concern tore at him, and he tenderly pushed her back to see her eyes. "Was I too rough? Did I hurt you?" He panicked at the sight of her tears.

She shook her head. "No." She sank onto the sofa beside them, and he sat down beside her. "You loved me so much in that kiss it literally moved me to tears."

He reached for her hand. "But it wasn't your first kiss?" He knew Lott Jenkins had likely kissed her, and he hated the thought.

She shook her head again. "Lott kissed me, if you could call it a kiss. He was rougher, harsher, and showed no tenderness or caring."

To his dismay, her tears started to fall harder. "You have no idea how much I wanted my first kiss to come from you, but I couldn't stop Lott. The whole time he kissed me, I thought of you so I wouldn't show my repulsion. I knew your kiss would be loving and gentle, so unlike his. What I didn't know is how passionate it would be or how it would make me ache for more. It t-transported me into a perfect place where only the two of us existed with God's blessing."

"Then I did give you your first kiss. If you found no pleasure in them, the others don't qualify as a kiss at all."

She smiled at him. "You always know what to say and do to make me feel my best. I feel whole and complete when I'm with you."

She had been so completely honest with him and told him her private thoughts that he wanted to do the same with her, but he needed some time to reflect on everything. This had been a life-changing day. And, if he didn't miss his guess, Melanie had begun to tire.

"You look like you're ready for bed. I'll have Gemona bring you supper in bed. Would you permit me to carry you upstairs?"

"I'd like that, but I don't want the day to end."

"What if I promise you another one just as good tomorrow?" And every day thereafter if he had his way.

"That would be a hard promise to keep. This one was so remarkable."

"Ah, but don't underestimate me."

She gave him a wide grin and lifted her arms to his neck. "All right, Sir Lucas, carry me away."

Lucas pulled her close and carried her up the steps. He eased her onto the bed, wishing he could just hold her as she slept. "I'll send Gemona up to help you get comfortable. Sweet dreams."

"Oh, they'll be sweet, all right."

He kissed her cheek. She made him feel like the most blessed man in the world and the richest one in ways that had nothing to do with wealth.

He left and went to his office, as much from habit as anything else. The last few days had been so freeing that he wondered why he'd stayed secluded at all. Melanie had been responsible for that, too.

Some did stare at him, but no one seemed repulsed as he'd imagined. Besides, if Melanie thought him handsome and gave him her love, it didn't matter what anyone else thought of him.

Glenna came sweeping in behind him, and he wondered if she'd been watching for him. "Melanie's reaction to your unveiling surprised you, didn't it?"

That didn't even begin to explain how he'd felt. "Did you come in here to gloat?"

Her smile widened. "I can't resist saying 'I told you so.'"

"You know what? I'm glad you were right and I was wrong on this. Gloat all you want. Melanie's worth any amount of groveling."

"And while we're on the subject, aren't you glad I coerced you into going to the masquerade ball?"

"Undeniably."

"So your old nanny still knows what's best for you?"

His generous mood would let Glenna have her moment of victory. Besides, if things went as planned, he might need an occasional nanny before too many more years. "Most of the time, she does."

"Then my advice to you is to marry the girl, and do it quickly."

"You don't have to try to talk me into that one. I'm in complete agreement."

Melanie thought herself too excited to sleep. Lott would no longer be a threat, William had approved of Lucas, and Lucas had truly been her knight. That kiss still left her breathless and weak every time she thought of it. There ought to be some other word to describe it, because "kiss" sounded much too common.

Lucas had almost made love to her in that kiss. If just one kiss left her feeling like this, what would a night with Lucas as his wife do to her? It was beyond her imagination.

Despite the thoughts skipping through her mind, not long after Lucas placed her on the bed, brushed his lips against her cheek, and closed the door, she drifted off.

Gemona woke her to get her to eat some supper. After she'd propped Melanie up in bed and placed a tray of food in her lap, she sat down. "I'm so happy for you."

"I'm glad we finally agree on a man for me."

Gemona laughed. "Yeah, well Toby would have been good, too. But I admit, for you, Lucas is much better."

"Speaking of Toby, I'm not sure what to do about him kidnapping us."

"He only meant to help you escape Lott, and everything did turn out for the best in the end, despite your accident. I've never seen you so happy."

Melanie nodded. "I've never been so happy."

"'Bout time, I'd say."

A light tap came at the door, and Melanie hoped she knew who that might be. When Gemona opened the door, Lucas came in with a tray of food. "I don't want to be presumptuous, but I would love to dine with you."

"I'm delighted to have you."

Gemona was already moving a small table close to the bed for him to set his tray on, and she left on the pretense of eating herself. In typical Gemona fashion, she left the bedroom door open behind her, but Melanie liked it that the rules governing proper behavior were more relaxed here than at William's.

Lucas kept the conversation light and carefree as they ate. He stood as soon as they'd finished and stacked her tray along with his. "I want you to get plenty of rest, and if you feel as if it won't be too strenuous for you, I'd like to take you riding in the morning. We won't go far, and we'll keep the pace slow and steady, but I think it might be good for you to get out in the fresh air."

"I'd love that. Looking forward to riding tomorrow almost makes your rushing away bearable."

He chuckled. "I love you so much, Melanie, I feel my chest may burst with it." He kissed her on the lips, but the short, quick kiss, though incredibly sweet, seemed little more than a peck.

When he closed the door, she closed her eyes. Maybe she could dream of a longer kiss.

Melanie woke early the next morning, eager for her morning with Lucas to start. Gemona helped her dress, and she went down at six-thirty, not expecting to see anyone but the cook but hoping there'd be hot water to steep some tea.

She met Lucas coming from the kitchen with a cup of coffee. His face lit up when he saw her. "You're up early."

She laughed. "I went to bed early."

"And slept well I hope."

"Yes, thank you." And had plenty of sweet dreams featuring Lucas, but she wouldn't tell him that.

They ate a leisurely breakfast, got on their horses, and rode out with Gemona following a ways behind. True to his word, Lucas held his horse back so they crept along.

"Can't we go a little faster?"

"Not this morning. I'm looking forward to dashing across the meadows with you, but you need to be patient and wait until you get stronger."

Well, at least he rode close beside her, and at this pace they could easily carry on a conversation. She looked around her. The heavy dew glistened in the sun, wildflowers dotted the fields, birds sang at the top of their voices, and an occasional frog croaked in the distance.

"Your estate is beautiful. How much land do you have?"

"Nearly twelve hundred acres."

"And you don't farm any of it?"

"No, I manage investments, which keep me busy, although we do have a large garden for our own use. I wouldn't be opposed to farming more, but without slaves, it would be harder to do."

They rode to the river. Its access looked even more open here than many of the areas around Winton, and it appeared wider here, too. In some ways, it didn't look like the same river.

Lucas helped her down from her horse, and held her hand as they meandered around. He pointed to a log. "Sometimes I come and go fishing."

"I grew up fishing in the Chowan. I still go sometimes, although I know it's not very ladylike."

"Really?" His eyebrow shot up, but he didn't look displeased. "You could never do anything that would make you look unladylike. Maybe we can come fishing tomorrow."

"I'd love that."

The morning passed much too fast, and Melanie reluctantly turned her horse back toward the house. "Thank you so much," she told him, as he lifted her to the ground.

"Believe me when I say the pleasure is all mine. We'll go in and eat dinner, and then I want you to take a long nap. The doctor is coming by sometime this afternoon, and I don't want his scolding if you look tired."

The doctor examined her and looked pleased. "I want you to continue to take an afternoon nap each day for about another month, but you're looking great. I don't see any lasting effects of your unconsciousness, and I'm going to release you from my care. Don't tax your strength, and let your body be your guide, but I'm not going to restrict you otherwise."

Fishing with Lucas turned out to be much better than fishing with anyone else. And the rest of their time together proceeded in idyllic days of spending as much time together as possible. Lucas planned something special for them each day, but Melanie didn't care what they did as long as she could be with Lucas.

William sent a slave with a note saying he would come to pick up Melanie on Friday. Constance would come with him this time, and they would stay the night. Constance would have a wet nurse to take care of Nancy. Melanie felt like crying when she went to bed that night – silly of her, because Lucas planned to come calling on her in Winton. Lucas had been secretive about his plans for Thursday. Maybe he had run out of ideas, but she doubted it. Knowing him, he most likely planned something special. Yet, time went by and they stayed inside most of the day.

They played some games of chess after Melanie got up from her nap. She won the first one, and Lucas won the other two.

At four o'clock they had a more substantial tea than usual. "We will likely dine later than usual this evening," Lucas told her.

When she went to dress for supper, Gemona had her best dress laid out. Made of white silk and trimmed in gold, it looked too dressy for supper, unless they were attending something she didn't know about. "What's going on?"

"I believe your beau has something special planned for you." Gemona's smug expression told Melanie the maid knew something she didn't plan to reveal.

Lucas met her at the bottom of the stairs wearing a tailored black frock coat over a gold vest. With his black pants and white shirt, he looked elegant, too.

"Are we going somewhere?"

"Only outside."

His answer puzzled her. Why would they dress up to just go outside?

He led her to the garden, and she had her answer. He had turned it into an even more magical place than the one in Edenton. With the flowers, brick walkway, and lanterns placed about at strategic locations, it looked enchanted.

He led her to a larger brick area with a small round table covered in a white linen tablecloth and with a gorgeous vase of flowers sitting in the center. Complete with table settings, she knew this would be where they'd dine. Lucas held her chair for her and then took the other.

"When did you do all this?"

"I've had the staff working on it for several days."

She could believe that it took several days. "Why?"

He took her hand. "I want our last night here together to be special, and I want to recreate that magical night when we met in Edenton."

"And Gemona?"

"Is out there somewhere, close enough to hear if you need something, but not keeping watch."

The staff served them and then disappeared. Melanie didn't even know what she ate, but it was delicious, and she guessed the dishes were French. Music played softly from a distance as they ate. He had thought of everything.

"I hate to think about leaving tomorrow."

"Not as much as I hate it." He kissed her hand. "But let's not let thoughts of tomorrow spoil the joy of tonight."

"You're right. These days of being with you have been the happiest I can ever remember. Thank you for that."

"You do realize you've given me back my life. Before you came and freed me from my self-imposed prison, I only half-existed. Ask Glenna. She'll tell you. You've put the pieces of my heart back together. You even led me back to God, but that's a tale for another time." He stood and extended his hand. "For now, could I please have this dance?"

She went into his arms gladly and they danced three straight waltzes. After the third one ended, he kissed her cheek. "Let's take a break."

He offered her his arm, and she took it. He put his other hand over hers.

They ambled down the pathway. The fragrance of flowers permeated the night. The heat of the day had cooled, and a soft breeze rustled the leaves.

He led her to a fountain surrounded by lush foliage and flowers and motioned for her to sit on a marble bench with a cushioned seat. He fell to his knees in front of her, and took both her hands in his. "Melanie, I never thought I'd ever find such happiness or love so completely. I don't know what I would ever do without you. Please say that you'll become my wife."

She couldn't believe he looked so uncertain of her answer. Didn't he know how much she adored him? He had her love, respect, and loyalty now and forever. "Yes. Yes, I'll marry you. I want you for my husband more than anything. You're already making all my dreams come true, and I'm looking forward to all our years together. "

He pulled her into his arms, and thanked her with a kiss that swept her away. Oh, yes, she wanted forever with Lucas Hall.

Chapter Twenty: Interlude

Melanie accompanied William and Constance back to Winton the next day. Constance had been more than impressed with Lucas and his estate. Melanie hadn't been sure how her sister-in-law would react to Lucas's scars, but she saw a man with a title and wealth, and that's all she could talk about.

"Well, most everything is in place from the wedding you missed," Constance told Melanie, "so it won't take much to have everything ready."

"I don't want any of the things we chose for me to wed Lott. I want all new, but I want to keep it simple, so I'm hoping none of it will take too long." Besides, she let Constance make the choices then, but she'd make these.

"You can't possible have a whole new trousseau made before September."

They'd set the wedding for September the third in the garden at Lucas's estate. "I don't need all that. Lucas will provide whatever I need later. Besides, don't underestimate my fiancé. If I wanted twenty seamstresses at my disposal, he'd see I had them."

That silenced Constance, and Melanie smiled to herself. The ride home seemed long, and she already fiercely missed Lucas.

When she walked in the house, she heard Nancy in the nursery. William already ran up the stairs, and Melanie followed. William took the baby from the nurse, and she hushed her fussing.

Melanie put out her hands. "Let me have a turn. I've never gotten to hold her at all."

The tiny girl looked up at Melanie with her baby blue eyes and cooed. "She's precious."

"I agree." William didn't try to hide his pride. "And she's already daddy's girl, aren't you sweetheart?" He peeped over at her in Melanie's arms and then glanced up at Melanie. "Hadn't you better be taking that nap the doctor ordered?"

Melanie laughed. "You're just trying to get Nancy away from me." But she handed the baby over. She hoped she'd have one of her own to hold in a year or so. The thoughts of having Lucas's child filled her with happiness.

Melanie had just come downstairs and started for the kitchen to check on afternoon tea, when Shadrack appeared. "Mr. Tobias Askew to see you, Miss," he said with his eyes grinning even though his mouth didn't.

"You know there's no need to be formal with Toby, you old rascal," she teased.

"It's good to have you back, Miss Melanie."

She didn't tell him it was good to be back, because she'd much rather be near Colerain. She started to rush to greet Toby but then slowed. How would he take the news of her wedding plans? She tried to swallow down her nervousness.

"Come into the parlor, and we can talk." She didn't look him in the eyes.

"Could we go outside instead, perhaps to the garden?"

"Sure." She led the way.

"Since Lott's now out of the picture, I'm marrying the man who's captured my heart." A little too abrupt perhaps, but they'd always been direct and honest with each other.

He didn't appear surprised or hurt. "I heard. Is it Lucas Hall?"

She nodded. "How did you know?"

"I helped arranged for you two to meet again."

"What do you mean?"

"The kidnapping. Gemona and I planned it, not only to get you away from Lott, but to let you escape on Hall's property. Gemona told me about you meeting him at the masquerade ball in Edenton, and how much you enjoyed his company. She said you called him your knight in shining armor. I want you to be happy, Mellie. If that takes Lucas Hall, then I wanted you to have him.

I took time off from the farm and managed to track him down. Then I led you in that direction and tied you up so you could escape."

Her eyes filled with tears. She'd spend part of her prayer time every day praying that Toby would find his happiness, too.

"Don't cry for me. I've found someone, too."

"Really?" She searched his face. If he just wanted to placate her, she'd know it.

"She's wonderful. Her name's Delphia Davis, and her hair's even redder than yours and brighter than fire. Her father has a small plantation towards Murfreesboro, and she's not opposed to being a farmer's wife."

His eyes lit up when he talked about the woman, and Melanie breathed a sigh of relief. "You're thinking of marrying her then?"

"I am. I think that's where this is headed, but I'll let you have your wedding first. However, I'll expect to be invited, and then you'd better come to mine."

"I will. I'm so happy for you."

"And I'm happy for you. We'll always stay best friends, won't we?"

"Of course. Lucas isn't the jealous type like Lott, and I think he's pretty sure of my love for him. In fact, I think you and he will be good friends, too."

"I also wanted to ask your forgiveness for kidnapping you. Gemona sort of talked me into it, and I couldn't come up with a better plan to get you away from Jenkins and to Hall. However, I almost worried myself to death when you were injured and lay in a coma."

"You're forgiven, although I don't think it was the wisest decision."

"I don't know. It did unite you with your knight."

"Yes, but God would have taken care of it. After all, the sheriff took Lott away."

Toby thought for a moment. "Sometimes God works through His people."

Melanie didn't think God approved of doing wrong, like kidnapping, but she didn't want to argue the point. Toby had tried to help her. And with Lucas withdrawing like he had, they may have never met again without Gemona's scheming. Right or wrong, her two friends had tried to come to her aid.

She sat there for a while longer after Toby took his leave. The enormity of what had transpired stunned her. But God had truly worked everything for good.

Three days later Lucas rode up as planned. Melanie didn't wait for him to come to the house. She went flying out the door to get to him as quickly as she could. He opened up his arms and she dashed into them.

"Oh how it does my heart good to have you run to me this way. You must have missed me about half as much as I've missed you, and half is still a lot. I've been so lonely without you."

She led him to the garden, wanting to spend some time alone with him before she had to share him with the others.

"Glenna wanted me to tell you we'll have everything ready for the wedding and the reception."

"I have no doubts that it'll be perfect. We've hired two extra girls to help Gemona with the sewing."

"You get anything you need, and I mean that. Buy anything, order anything, or hire anyone. I don't want you worrying about any of it."

"The only thing I'm worrying about is being away from you until September the third."

She told him about Toby's visit. "Do you think God really wanted Toby to kidnap me?"

"I don't know, although like you, I question it. But we don't have to judge him and Gemona, do we? We can leave that up to God. I'd almost talked myself into letting Glenna bandage my face and coming to try to rescue you. If William wanted financial security, I could offer it."

"You're right and it's a moot point anyway. We're together and planning to wed, and that's what matters. Toby and his family will be at the wedding, and I'm looking forward to you meeting him. I think you two will like each other."

"Should I be jealous?" He looked like he teased, and she hoped so.

She laughed. "Not of anyone. Ever. I've waited for you my whole life, and you have my complete love and loyalty. I think Constance had started to worry that I'd be a spinster. I could have married Toby to escape Lott, but I refused. He deserved a wife who loved him differently than as a sister, and I decided to hold out for God's best for me and trust Him to bring it."

His eyes held so much warmth and affection Melanie almost forgot to breathe. "Your faith amazes me." She saw his sincerity.

"You said one time that I helped bring you back to God. How did I do that?"

He proceed to tell how he'd heard her argument with Lott on the ship deck in Edenton and felt compelled to pray for her, although he'd had nothing to do with God since Margaret Ann rejected him and married his brother.

"God really does use bad situations to bring some good, doesn't He?"

"I'm seeing that more and more. I wouldn't have come to America without my scars, and I wouldn't have met you. Therefore I can rejoice in them because of that."

She nodded, glad that he could see it that way. "I have some good news." She changed the subject. "William has agreed to let me come to Colerain two weeks before the wedding in order to make preparations, since we're holding the wedding there. Then he and Constance will come two days before it."

Melanie looked at the house and saw Gemona sitting outside on a bench by the backdoor sewing and doing her chaperone duties. "I guess I should invite you in, although I'd like nothing more than to keep you to myself."

He grinned. "You always have me, darling, wherever we are. Even when we're apart, you're always in my thoughts."

She looked at his lips wanting to feel them on hers, but she knew they should wait. If he kissed her now, she might never make it inside.

Although Lucas stayed overnight, the time sped by, and she walked him to the stable via the garden as he readied to leave. She clung to him as he told her how much he loved her and how much he would miss her in a kiss. She answered him in the way she kissed him back.

"It won't be long now, since you'll be coming two weeks early, but I'll come again to visit next week."

"All right," she whispered, although it wasn't at all satisfactory. It wouldn't be until they didn't have to part again.

The time for Melanie to leave for Colerain did finally come. William called her into his office the evening before she left. "I'm glad to see you so happy, Mel, but I still hate to see you go."

"I'm not going all that far. Lucas and I will come and visit, and I expect you and Constance to do the same. I don't want to miss out on seeing Nancy grow up."

"Here." He handed her some official looking papers. "Lucas purchased these for you."

She looked down and she held the papers for Gemona and Jericho. "Lucas bought them?"

William looked down in embarrassment. "I had planned to give you Gemona as a wedding present, but Lucas insisted on buying both of them and gave me top price.

Melanie grinned, knowing that the two slaves would soon be freed. Yet, she also knew they'd choose to stay on Lucas's estate. Gemona would be as lost without Melanie as Melanie would be without the maid. And Jericho had been loyal to both her and Gemona through the years. In fact, if she didn't miss her guess, Gemona and Jericho had an interest in each other that might come to light once Melanie had married and no longer needed Gemona as much.

"Thank you, William, and I'll thank Lucas when I see him."

"Yes, and we'll see you two before long. Constance is really looking forward to our visit."

William had remained seated behind his desk, so Melanie stepped around it and kissed his cheek. He had provided for her for a number of years, and tried to be both parent and brother to her.

The servants loaded her things while she ate breakfast, and they were on the road by eight-thirty. She couldn't wait to see Lucas, and she felt as if she was returning home. That's what his estate had become to her, but then, wherever Lucas was would be home.

He came out to meet her carriage and helped her down into his arms. "Welcome home, darling." He knew it, too.

Although Glenna wanted Melanie's approval on the plans she and Lucas had made, all but the last minute details had been taken care of, and that freed her to spend most of her time with Lucas. She couldn't have been happier.

"With us getting married so soon after I proposed, I'm sorry you haven't been courted the way you deserve." This time Lucas looked serious, and didn't seem to be teasing.

"I can't believe you said that. You've courted me every time you've seen me since you took the bandage off your face. Just the way you look at me courts me, and you've done so much more than that. Why, one of your kisses is worth a thousand days of courtship."

"Do you really think so?"

"I know so."

He smiled, picked her up, and twirled her around. When he released her, he sat her down so close to him that they almost touched. "You make me feel whole despite my deformities and fill me with joy."

"Besides, I think it will be even better to be courted by my husband with no restrictions as to what is and isn't allowed."

She felt her face begin to flush. She moved into him, knowing he'd wrap her in his arms and she could hide her reddening cheeks in his chest.

He kissed the top of her head. "Then I'm glad we didn't wait longer. I'm having a hard time waiting for that day myself."

They broke apart, he took her hand, and they began walking toward the garden where he wanted to show her the wooden arch he'd had built for them to stand in front of while they said their vows. She didn't know how he'd gotten so many red roses to trail over it, but she had begun to realize that Lucas could make things happen.

The garden had never looked lovelier, and she didn't want to know how many gardeners he'd had working here to get everything just right. "Lucas, you don't have to go to such pains to make everything perfect. Marrying you makes it about as perfect as it can get."

His face darkened with concern. "You don't like it? Tell me what you want, and I'll see to it."

She put her hand on his arm. "I love it. But I want you to know that you are what matters to me." She swung her hand around to indicate the garden. All this doesn't matter nearly as much, and as long as I end up with you, everything will be perfect for me."

"You really mean that, don't you?" His stare penetrated her.

"With all my heart. Lott wanted to give me a lavish, extravagant wedding that most women would have loved, but I hated it, because he was the wrong man. You and I could get married in a run-down shack and I would love it, because you're the right man."

"And my scars don't disgust you?" His eyes hadn't left her face.

"No. They only bother me in that I hate to think of what you've had to endure. I still think you're the most handsome man I've ever met."

He gave a laugh that held little humor. "How can that be?"

"It's hard to explain. Let me just say that the left side of your face is so handsome, that when you average it with the right side of your face, you still come out more handsome than anyone I've ever seen. But it's this," she patted his chest, "that I fell in love with. You have the most beautiful heart of anyone I've ever met."

"It's only you who sees it that way."

"No, it's not. I'm sure Glenna would agree with me. Besides, who else's opinion is more important to you?"

He laughed. "You are absolutely right, sweetheart, and I'm glad you are willing to keep me straight."

She looked at him and smiled sweetly. "Will you take me riding again soon, now that we don't have to inch along because of my injuries?"

"How about tomorrow morning?"

"Perfect. Thank you."

Chapter Twenty-One: The Finale

During the day, with Melanie close, Lucas didn't doubt that she loved him. The way her eyes lit up when he walked into the room and softened when he drew near to her, the way she melted into his arms every time he hugged her, the way he had her rapt attention when he spoke, and the way she responded to his kisses all told him so. But at night, alone in his bedroom, Lucas had a hard time believing that Melanie could want someone like him for a husband.

Unlike Margaret Ann, he knew she wasn't just interested in his money or his English title, but he didn't see that he had anything else to offer. However, if Melanie didn't care about status and wealth, didn't that have to mean that she just wanted him? He couldn't understand it.

In those dark moments he vowed that he'd do everything in his power to make sure she never regretted marrying him. He loved spoiling her and treating her special.

Lucas awoke as soon as the daylight started lightening the room. He got up immediately, knowing that Melanie would be eager to go riding this morning, and would likely be up early, too.

He looked back at his empty bed. He couldn't wait until Melanie would sleep there beside him, but he tried to not dwell on that now. Considering how wonderful it felt to touch her and hold her and how passionate their kisses had been from the very first one, he needed to think about other things until their wedding night. He loved and respected her too much to do otherwise.

By the time he shaved, dressed, and made it to the dining room, Melanie sat sipping a cup of tea. "You're up early."

"I can hardly wait to go riding."

"Oh, are you going riding today?"

"Lucas, don't tease like that. I've been looking forward to it ever since you promised."

He grinned. "Truth be told, so have I. Jericho said he would have our horses ready this morning."

Melanie nodded. "He's a good worker, don't you think? He can do almost anything and filled in wherever we needed him."

"He seems to be, and I'm already having the papers drawn up to free him and Gemona."

"Thank you. I'm glad. I know Gemona wants to stay on as my maid, and I'm assuming Jericho will want to work for you, too."

Lucas nodded. "He told me as much."

They ate their breakfast and went outside to mount their horses. He helped Melanie onto her sidesaddle, hoping she would be secure enough, because he had a feeling she planned to go racing across the meadow.

They started off at a trot, but soon followed with a gallop. Then Melanie nudged her horse and flew out front, calling over her shoulder, "Race you to the river."

With his favorite horse bigger and stronger than Melanie's mare, he had no trouble catching up, but he stayed beside her instead of pulling ahead.

He had dreamed of this – riding side by side with her, the wind in their faces. They glided over the ground, one with the animals, one with each other.

When the river grew nearer, he let his horse have a slight lead before they drew up. Her voice rang out in laughter. "That was so much fun. I know you could have won by several horses' lengths, but I loved riding beside you like that. I felt free and alive and blessed."

He jumped from his horse and scooped her from her saddle. He needed her in his arms.

As far as Lucas was concerned, she pulled away too soon but put her hand in his and led him toward the river. She stood looking out at the flowing water. "I like the river. It seems vital and alive."

She turned to smile at him, but froze. In an instant, her eyes were wide with fear. "No-o-o!"

He just barely turned in time to see a knife aimed at him. He dodged by reflex. "Run!" He shouted to

Melanie, but his eyes never left the man with the knife. "Go get help," he added, hoping that would get her out of harm's way.

She headed for her horse but stopped and turned, now to the side and slightly behind the man. "Don't do this, Lott."

Jenkins? This was Lott Jenkins?

"You're mine, Melanie, and you'll always be mine. I came for you before I head to England." The man's eyes didn't glance Melanie's way but remained on Lucas.

"I'm not going anywhere with you."

Lucas wished Melanie would just go back to the house, so he'd know she was safe. But then maybe she couldn't get on the horse with all those skirts without help.

"I heard you were planning to marry someone else. Surely you aren't planning to marry this monster."

"Lucas knows how to treat a lady. In that regard, you're the monster, Lott."

"I'll show you." Jenkins gave a slight twist of his head to glance back a Melanie, and Lucas made his move. He caught the man's wrist before he had time to bring it forward. The surprise attack caused Jenkins to drop the knife, but the man's strength surprised Lucas.

Jenkins fought like a raging bull, but Lucas's agility and quickness kept most of the punches from making contact, and he fought smarter. He finally saw an opening and punched Jenkins hard, knocking him to the ground and rendering him unconscious. Jericho came rushing up followed by three other men. "Dis here's the sheriff," the slave said. He turned to Melanie. "You's all right, Miss Melanie?"

"I am now." She came up to stand beside Lucas, and he took her hand.

"Jenkins escaped on the way to the courthouse," the sheriff said after introductions were made. "We've been tracking him for days. I thought he might try to make it back to Winton, because I had a feeling he'd want to see Miss Carter, but when I heard she was here planning a wedding, we came."

"I'm glad you did, Lucas said. You are welcome to him."

The sheriff chuckled. "You did the hard part, so my job is easy this time."

The other two men had already tied up Jenkins, but he came to enough to walk to a horse. He didn't say a word to anyone but gave them all looks that could kill, especially Lucas and Melanie.

"Don't worry about him." The sheriff stared at Jenkins and shook his head. "He won't get away again, and the judge will be twice as hard on him now."

"Are you ready to go back, darling?"

"Yes." She touched the corner of his mouth. "I was so frightened for you there for a while, because I know what a brute Lott can be, but you handled him quite well. However, we do need to get you back and take care of your few cuts, although you look remarkable well for a man who's been in a fight."

"We sure don't want them to leave scars now, do we?"

"That's not funny."

He thought it was. "Isn't it good that I can laugh about them now? I couldn't for a long time."

"I'll not have you sarcastically disparaging my knight in any way." Her eyes danced in merriment.

"Your knight is upset that he didn't get to kiss you by the river."

"Then he'll just have to kiss me twice to make up for it."

Glenna clucked over him like a mother hen as she washed his nicks. "What's this world coming to when a man can't even take his fiancée on a ride on his own property without being accosted?"

"To no good, I'd say." He'd play along with her tirade for now.

"Watch him." Melanie came up behind him and put her hands on his shoulders. "He's in the mood to tease, and he's shameless with it."

"Well, he can tease me all he wants." Glenna must have decided to take his side for a change. "I saw nothing but long faces and dark moods from him for such a long time that it's good to have the happy man back."

Melanie gave his shoulders a squeeze before withdrawing and looking at his face. Her smiled warmed him.

"There now. There shouldn't be a sign of a fight by the wedding." Glenna took her basin of water and cloth and headed for the backdoor.

Glenna's last remark reminded Lucas of what he'd said earlier about the scars, and he almost burst into laughter.

"Don't you dare." Melanie must have read his mind.

He got up and put his arm around her waist to lead her into the parlor. "Then come talk to me of something else and get my mind off it all."

Lucas liked the rhythm of his days with Melanie here. She made life both exciting and enjoyable. William and Constance came, and that disrupted things somewhat, but it also meant that the day for the wedding would soon be there.

September the third dawned clear without even a red sky to give warning. Lucas had worried about what they would do if it rained. They had backup plans to hold it inside if need be, but it didn't look like they would need them.

Toby Askew arrived early. Melanie gave him a happy hug the moment she saw him, and Lucas experienced a moment of jealousy before he chided himself. He knew very well he had her heart. He found he actually liked Askew. He should have known Melanie's friend would be a good man.

"Tssk." Constance shook her head at Melanie. "Lucas shouldn't be seeing you before the wedding. It's unlucky."

"I'm not in my wedding dress yet." Melanie tried to reason.

"There is nothing ever unlucky about me seeing Melanie. She blesses me with her presence." Lucas wanted to support Melanie. It would have been a long morning if he couldn't have seen her.

Constance didn't say anything, but she went off still shaking her head.

When Melanie went upstairs to get ready well before the appointed time, Lucas found himself thankful for William and Constance's help. As more guests arrived, the day became a whirlwind of activity. They hadn't invited many people, but the nearly forty guests who came seemed more like four hundred to Lucas. No one appeared openly rude or disgusted with his disfigured face, but he received many surprised stares. He just reminded himself of all the things Melanie had said and brushed off the adverse reactions. He wasn't going to let anything spoil the day he made Melanie his wife.

He appreciated his staff more today than ever, because the day proceeded as he'd hoped with no snags or problems. He wanted to give Melanie the wedding of her dreams, one she could look back on with pleasure as the years progressed. He smiled to himself. He wanted to grow old with her, raise a family, and live the rest of his life with her close by his side. *Thank you, Lord, for all Thy many blessings.*

Nervous excitement filled Melanie, and she was glad she had Gemona to help her get ready. The day had finally come when she could marry Lucas, the man of her dreams, her knight in shining armor.

He and Glenna had taken care of all the details, and she'd had to do very little. Her and Lucas's tastes were so similar and he organized and handled details so well that she had no doubt everything would be perfect. Just the days they'd spent together leading up to this had been as idyllic. Not even Lott's unwanted appearance could mar her joy.

"I sure haven't seen much of you since you've been with Lucas." Regret filled Gemona's voice.

"Are you sorry you manipulated events to bring us back together?" Melanie only half-teased.

A wide grin spread across Gemona's face. "Are you serious? I know how happy you are with your knight, and I'm happy for you. I hope you do realize now that I did help you out."

They had discussed their differing view on the kidnapping, and Melanie didn't want to get back into it today. "I am happy." What an understatement.

"Sometime, I'd like to talk to you about Jericho and me."

"Really? I've suspected you two might have feelings, but I wasn't sure. That's wonderful. When you're ready we can arrange a wedding right here if you'd like."

"Slaves don't get legally married, but I'd like to have a small ceremony anyway if you don't mind."

"You aren't a slave anymore, and I'm sure Lucas can arrange a legal marriage for you. He knows how to make things happen and get things done."

The smile came back to Gemoma's face. "Yes, he does. That man is something else."

Looking in the mirror after Gemona finished, she wondered what Lucas would think. The striking contrast of the sapphire blue silk with its white trim looked strikingly bold but matched her blue eyes and provided a good background for her bright hair. And Gemona had done a good job with her hair, putting it up in curls with some hanging in just the right places.

A knock came at the door, and Melanie looked at the time. Surely William hadn't already come to collect her. But when Gemona opened the door, Glenna stood there with a box in her hands. "Lucas sent these to you. He said you didn't have to wear them, but he wanted you to have them today. They're the only thing of value he has left from his mother."

"Melanie opened them to find an unusual set of sapphires and diamonds, accented with a sprinkling of pearls."

"They're beautiful. How did he know what I was wearing today?"

"I'm not sure he did, although he has a way of finding out whatever information he wants. That's what has made him so successful with his investments. He has doubled his assets since taking over this estate a few years ago."

"Tell him I'm very pleased."

"I will, but I'll leave it to you to thank him later." Glenna left with Melanie wondering just what she meant. Her statement could be taken several different ways.

When she put on the necklace, earrings, and bracelet, they went with her gown beautifully. Now she did feel like a queen.

William came to get her not long afterwards. "You look stunning," he told her.

He led her to the garden, but they stood out of view until their signal came. She heard the musicians playing in the background.

When the right chords sounded, they stepped out. Her eyes hurriedly took in the view – the lush flowers and plants, the guests sitting on padded benches with lace and ribbons, the arch of roses up front, the preacher, and then Lucas.

He stood with his left side showing, and he took her breath away. He turned his head toward her as she started down the aisle made by the six rows of benches on each side, and his eyes met hers and held them. They told her everything she needed to know, and she didn't see anything else but him.

The minister kept the ceremony short. He read from 1 Corinthians 13 and spoke a few words of wisdom. She and Lucas said their vows looking at each other. Lucas placed a ring on her finger that matched the other jewelry she wore, and she hadn't expected that. She needed to start expecting him to do wonderful things she hadn't anticipated.

When the minister announced them husband and wife and Lucas kissed her, he didn't just give her a demure kiss as most would have done with an audience watching. Instead his kiss held all the promise and love he wanted to show her, and she clung to him.

The reception followed, and the musicians moved into the house. She and Lucas greeted everyone, but Melanie planned to go back and talk with some of them more. For now, Glenna had excelled herself, and the food beckoned everyone.

"I've never seen you look lovelier, dear." Mrs. Askew patted Melanie's hand. "And it's not just that gorgeous dress and magnificent jewelry. There's a glow about you that radiates happiness."

"Lucas is good for me."

Lucas bent toward the older lady. "Don't let her fool you. I'm the blessed one."

Mrs. Askew laughed. "As long as you both keep thinking like that, you'll have a successful marriage for sure. But come. I want you to meet Toby's love interest. I don't think you've got to meet her yet."

Melanie took Lucas's arm so that he would come, too, and she didn't have to urge him. He didn't want to leave her side either.

Delphia Davis turned out to be a pretty woman with flaming red hair, and eyes as green as summer grass. The generous smattering of freckles across her nose and cheeks kept her from being a beauty, but Melanie liked her, and she could tell Toby did, too.

"You have a good man there." Melanie nodded toward Toby. "He's always been a dear, faithful friend, and I know he'll make someone a wonderful husband."

Toby looked away in embarrassment, but Delphia laughed. "You're not telling me anything I don't know. I think he's wonderful."

That brought a smile to Toby's face. "Save me one dance, Mellie. For old time's sake."

"I'll do that for you, but, with the exception of William, all the other dances are reserved for Lucas."

"Speaking of which," Lucas told her, "I think everyone is waiting for us to lead it off."

He took her to the dance floor and pulled her into his arms. "I love dancing with you," she whispered.

"I've loved it from our first dance in Edenton, and I've danced with you a hundred times in my dreams."

"And a hundred more in mine."

"She danced with William next and then with Toby. "You were right," Toby told her. "What we felt for each other was more like what twins feel. I felt so close to you, and I did love you fiercely, but it wasn't the romantic love it should have been for marriage. I realize that now. But we will remain friends, won't we?"

She knew that meeting Delphia had shown him the truth. "Absolutely. I like Delphia, and I can tell Lucas likes you. I think the four of us will remain close friends."

When Lucas claimed her for the fourth dance, she knew she'd not dance with anyone else. "Let's sneak out to the garden and leave a back door open so we can hear the music."

They waltzed in the garden and being alone in the outdoor setting made it even more special. "Let's slip away now." Lucas's voice trembled with emotion.

"All right."

Their horses stood ready, and Jericho and three other hands would escort them to the river with lanterns where they would board Lucas's ship. Their trunks had already been taken there. They'd spend the night on the ship and set sail tomorrow. After some time in the rest of Europe, they'd set sail for England where Lucas hoped to make peace with his brother.

"I don't begrudge him Margaret Ann," Lucas had told her. "Things have worked out much better for me than for him. I want to tell them both that I forgive them."

From what Melanie had heard of Margaret Ann, she knew that the woman wouldn't have made Lucas happy and wondered if his brother didn't already regret marrying her. In addition, the way Glenna talked about Margaret Ann's spending she imagined Lucas had more wealth now, too. But she was proud that Lucas wanted to make amends, and it would be his final act of moving out of his past.

The lighted ship sitting on the river looked magical in the darkness. Lucas pulled her off the horse so her body brushed against the length of him as he slowly let her feet touch the ground. He scooped her up and carried her to the small boat that would take them out to the ship, reminding her of the first time he'd done that when she'd been injured.

Since Gemona hated sailing, Lucas told her he would hire her a lady's maid when they got to Europe. In the meantime, aboard the ship, he could take care of anything for her that she couldn't do herself. She smiled at that thought.

When they got to their cabin door, he picked her up again and carried her over the threshold. She barely had time to look over the huge room that he must have had enlarged for this voyage before his lips met hers with an eagerness that spurred her passion. This time she didn't have to hold anything back, and she could respond to him with abandonment.

Melanie woke up in Lucas's arms, and he tugged her closer when he saw she was awake. "Hm-m. I like waking up like this."

His smile warmed her even more, because his eyes told her how much he loved her. "How do you feel?" He stroked her cheek.

"Too happy to describe. I feel overflowing with love – both mine for you and yours for me."

"I know what you mean. This has been the most remarkable courtship ever, and I see the marriage is going to be even more spectacular."

She leaned up on an elbow so she could see his face better. "All because of you."

"Whatever I've done right, it's because I had you to inspire me." His look of adoration melted her through and through.

She wouldn't argue with him, but she knew she had received the bigger blessing when he came into her life. "And to think, it all started at the masquerade."

He smothered any other words with a kiss that drew her into their special world, and his touch pushed away anything but the sensations he caused.

For more information about

Janice Cole Hopkins

Web page: www.JaniceColeHopkins.blogspot.com

Email: wandrnlady@aol.com

Twitter: @J_C_Hopkins

Facebook: www.facebook.com/JaniceColeHopkins
(Please like this author's page)

If you enjoyed the book, please leave a review on Amazon and/or similar sites to let others know. This is the best way to say "Thank you" to an author.

All the author's profits go to a scholarship fund for missionary children

Made in the USA
Middletown, DE
01 February 2018